Watch for more Bramble Patch Books

by M.L. Joslyn

from Indigo Sea Press

indigoseapress.com

Try Me On

By

M.L. Joslyn

Bramble Patch Books
Published by Indigo Sea Press
Winston-Salem

Bramble Patch Books
Indigo Sea Press
302 Ricks Drive
Winston-Salem, NC 27103

First Bramble Patch Books edition published

February, 2016

Bramble Patch Books, Moon Sailor and all production design are trademarks of Indigo Sea Press, used under license.

For information regarding bulk purchases of this book, digital purchase and special discounts, please contact the publisher at indigoseapress.com

Cover design by Pan Morelli

Manufactured in the United States of America
ISBN 978-1-63066-291-2

Chapter One

A string of young women leaned against the broad checkout counter clutching their precious bargains. Jack Timmons monitored the early-evening activity from his vaguely obscured post on the sales floor amidst three round racks of clearance blouses and a t-stand loaded with gaudy, yet for some reason very popular, sundresses. He was beaming.

With each peep of his store's money-gobbling cash registers, Jack's annual bonus would fatten a little. The thirty-year-old manager looked forward to collecting, and then wasting, his five-figure, end-of-year, atta-boy reward, but that didn't account for his joyous mood; he was shallower than that. He owed his conspicuously smug grin to the thinly veiled mass of curvy, firm butts pivoting just feet from his position.

The line of foot shuffling, nubile shoppers patiently awaited their turn to pay, while carefully curated, wallet-lubricating background music spilled from well-hidden speakers. The huddle of alluring asses bobbed and danced as if encouraged by more than the muted tunes. These tantalizing babes pawed through their purses for credit cards, loose bills, or, just as likely, pieces of strawberry-kiwi bubble gum. Each one of the fledgling beauties was more delicious than the next. And, fortunately for Jack, they all loved to shop at J. Annie's, the hottest discount fashion store in Phoenix.

"Jack?" Julie Wendelsohn, the store's assistant manager, had been flitting and twirling around her disconcertingly focused boss for a minute, hoping he'd notice.

"What? Oh, hey Julie. Looks like another great day, huh? Corporate will be pleased."

"Yeah. I hope they're as pleased as you seem to be. Listen, I want to talk to you about Joel. I've had a number of comments from the girls about him hanging around the fitting room curtains. Kind of creeps them out. I was hoping you could deal with this?"

"Joel's our stock supervisor, Julie. How's he supposed to keep the store merchandised if he's not allowed on the sales floor?"

1

Although Joel was a bit awkward, and sometimes a little slow on the uptake, Jack appreciated his diligence and saw no reason to come down hard on the indefatigable young worker. Besides, he was the only other male store employee. As much as Jack enjoyed sloshing about in a sea of females, he liked having another guy around who he could share the inevitable anecdotes, or marvel at the concept of community fitting rooms with. "Maybe I'll remind him to focus only on the racks outside the fitting rooms."

Julie rolled her eyes then tromped back to her office to finish working on the weekly staff schedule. Jack remained glued to his post, or box seat, as he liked to think of it, shifting his scrutiny toward his retreating assistant manager. Without Julie's help he'd be a hopeless square peg, lost in a job he should never have qualified for. She had the fashion knowledge he lacked. He had a strong retail management background—in sporting goods, not women's apparel. A year ago, Jack might have fallaciously proclaimed Dolce & Gabbana his favorite brand of gelato in an overhasty attempt to impress. But Julie would bail him out, time after time. He didn't understand why she came to his rescue so often, but he appreciated it, and he appreciated her.

Jack's gaze remained tacked to Julie's swinging, narrow hips as she navigated the crammed aisles on her way to the office. Since the day they met, the day Jack was ceremoniously shepherded into the store by Mike Allen, the district manager, and introduced as the new store manager, Jack had wanted to touch her, play with her...take her for a test drive. But there were rules against such things. Corporate had little tolerance for hanky-panky between a store manager and his or her assistant. Jack was certain that buttoned-down Julie had zero tolerance.

Still, she was a twenty-six year old petite cutie with short blonde hair, modest, firm tits, and a shapely, compact ass. And Jack was a single guy who found each of those attributes irresistible. If only she wasn't such a goody two-shoes, he thought.

It's not that Jack was interested in a serious relationship. He'd already been down that alley, taken that bait. His bruises were still fading beneath his unguarded skin, an ex-girlfriend having delivered the impolite blow, or, more accurately, unleashing, a year earlier.

***

"So, what are you going to do now?" Rebecca Goodwin affected an attitude precisely between total concern and not giving a shit.

"Obviously I've got to find a new job, Beck. I'm pretty sure you're not up for being my sugar momma." Jack scrutinized Rebecca's face searching for any indication that his girlfriend of almost three years might, for the first time ever, recognize sarcasm.

"You know I can't support you, Jack. The money I don't need for essentials goes to pay off my student loans." Rebecca dripped lotion down her legs, signaling the start of her nightly pre-bed ritual.

"I wasn't asking you to bail me out. You asked me a question, and I…never mind."

The sudden, edgy silence of the room was interrupted by the lewd, sloppy sounds of creamy moisturizer slogging into even creamier skin. Jack never tired of watching his girlfriend tackle her more intimate chores—especially when she was quiet like this. Of course, she needed to keep up her daily regimen of total body maintenance; her amazing looks were all she had, really. Jack was embarrassed to admit it, but if she were just slightly less hot, he would have left her long ago. Now it was only a question of time. Once she'd had enough of him and his derisive asides, they both would get on with their lives. And so he took advantage of these fugitive moments, soaking up the view, snapping mental keepsakes.

"Why don't you just get another store manager job? You seem to be good at that—I guess." Rebecca's long fingers drifted dotingly over her strong, bronze thighs.

"Retail's all I know, Beck, so I suppose that's what I'll do. I'm not sure what's out there, though." Jack continued to lean closer to his rancorous girlfriend until he was at just the right angle above her. As far as he could tell, she was oblivious to his proximity.

All that separated Jack from a naked Rebecca was a pair of stretchy, pink-dyed shorts, that, aside from the gentle, pastel hue, could be mistaken for men's boxer briefs purchased two sizes too small. Jack scrutinized her amazing rack for about the gazillionth time as she leaned forward to smear lotion on her ankles.

Back when they were first dating, Rebecca was all about the sex, needing it often and wanting it in ways Jack had presumed exclusive

3

to hardcore porn. She would often beg him to slide his seven inches between her tits and pump away, her head tilting forward to catch the view and inevitable rush of warm "Jack candy," one of her many uncomfortable, yet ego fostering labels for his streaming release. The girl with an unabating sexual hunger would then suck his fading hard-on while fingering herself to feverish spasms of her own.

Sometimes, Rebecca would secure Jack's wrists to whatever was convenient, like a nearby coffee table, or stair railing, or even a steering wheel, using her panties as a tether; she was an exceptionally well-trained girl scout. Then, after stripping down to just skin, she'd pull from her serious collection of dildos, vibrators, and erotic toys that only a warped woman or mechanical engineer might comprehend, and have at herself while he watched. She liked him to have a good, close look at the action, too. Her mound would transform into the lead of some unthinkable, in your face, one-woman show, and he would be assigned the best seat in the house, on stage, inches from the weeping heroine. Jack would stare, corded to whatever station Rebecca had commissioned for him, soaking up the frenzy of unmasked drama. Rebecca's pussy would unfold from its bunched up, complicated mash of carnal paradise, prodded by one, or more, of her purposeful, persistent tools. Her yawning lips would latch on to whichever of her devices, sucking them in, then spitting them out. An obvious, slick sheen would glaze the fortunate appliance. For Jack, it was a pat on his back, a measure of his worth to her; after all, he knew she would not be so wet, so turned on, without him as her special audience.

When Jack's hard dick would begin to pulse like a ticking time bomb, Rebecca would give him what he wanted. Planking over his body, she'd allow her button-hard nipples to traverse his lips—right, left, right—until her weighty breasts would succumb to gravity and fall to his chest, compressed against his fevered skin. Grazing his steely erection with her prancing twat, she'd continue to taunt him before allowing him in. The tip of his prick would moisten with her juices, and she'd slide back to have a taste of him and her at once. Sometimes, he would lose it right then, bold spurts of his come recklessly painting her face. Sometimes, he would make it inside her warm, moist hole, at least for a few strokes, before releasing his bullied load.

4

But that was before. Before sex had become a chore, or Jack had become a bore, or whatever it was that had turned Rebecca from a sex fiend to a wintry marble slab.

"My friend Laurie has an interview for a management position with J. Annie's next week. She's an idiot; can barely manage her own life. You should check into it." Rebecca planted tiny dabs of lotion between her toes as she spoke. Jack kept one hand over his ungovernable crotch.

"Gee, thanks for the compliment, Beck. But, J. Annie's, that's a woman's clothing store, isn't it? I'm pretty sure even your idiot friend would be more qualified to work there than me. I'll try to find another sporting goods gig, or something I might understand."

"You're a store manager, Jack. At the end of the day, does it really matter how many bowling balls you've sold?"

"I understand bowling balls. I don't understand women." A sluggish light plowed into Jack's brain like a cold, dragging, CFL bulb. The little she-devil was after his employee discount—potential employee discount.

"Hey, I'm just trying to help. Personally, I'm not a big fan of the store. You have to use one of their community fitting rooms if you want to try anything on. They're huge, mirror covered spaces, so you can't change clothes without like twenty other women watching. Sometimes, it can be, like, really gross. Anyway, Laurie found the job opening on their website. Couldn't hurt to take a look, could it?"

Jack spun away from his relationship-status photo of a girlfriend, shuffled from the room, and fell backwards onto his bed. He stared at a featureless, beige ceiling, assembling his thoughts. If a man could appear slump shouldered while lying down, he'd nailed it.

Jack's laptop, recharging from an unintended World of Warcraft marathon, warmed a thin, rumpled blanket at the foot of the bed. His ankle bumped against it and he sat up to make sure he hadn't pushed it too close to the edge. *Couldn't hurt to take a look, could it?* What a bitch. It was no use fighting her self-serving request. Jack opened his browser and Googled J. Annie's. A few seconds later he was clicking through pages of smiling, hot young women, all apparently happy as hell to be wearing the retailer's hemmed-at-the-ass dresses and tops that flaunted more breast than fabric. The trendy clothes looked like they had been plucked straight from Rebecca's closet.

Before closing the site and moving on to something more relevant, like researching the new pizza joint up the road, Jack clicked the About Us button at the top of J. Annie's home page. The mind-numbing information it dispensed confirmed to him that he had just wasted the last two minutes of his life. He could care less that J. Annie's was the fastest growing young-ladies fashion discounter in the country, or that they were stockpiling Best Of awards like Costco stocked toilet paper.

But there it was, tucked at the bottom of the page, under the heading: Who We Are. It was a list of company executives. And they were all men. Maybe Chris, the Vice President of marketing, was a woman, but considering the rest of the list was populated with George's, Larry's, Bill's, and Greg's, it was doubtful. *What the hell?*

Jack hunted for the employment opportunities page, found the listing, and then pondered his next move. He was pretty sure he didn't even qualify for an interview. And if he did, his unmistakable lack of enthusiasm for the position would certainly offset his awesomely embellished resume.

Rebecca had been pretty passionate about having Jack chase after this job. He considered that if he put forth a little effort and applied for it, she might be inspired to put forth a little something, like applying her lips to his cock, perhaps. There was always some weird shit or other traversing Rebecca's mind. Her little fantasy of a permanent, double-digit discount might be the key to unlocking her frisky mode, he thought. Jack had heard tales of women getting all juiced up just by contemplating a cute pair of jeans. What if their boyfriends had access to whole stores of them? He could only imagine.

Jack cobbled together a fresh cover letter, dusted the meaningless, part-time jobs he had held in college from his resume, and sent the file into the cloud, where someone in J. Annie's human resources department would retrieve it, compact it to a negligible size, and toss it into their electronic trashcan. Or so he had assumed.

The irony of the whole thing was that Rebecca had led him to this job—shoved it down his throat, really. And yet, J. Annie's was just like a nightclub that served only chocolate-strawberry martinis, or a theater that screened only Channing Tatum flicks, or an astrology convention. There were girls everywhere. There was sex everywhere. And for the longest time, Rebecca had been sex nowhere.

Three days before Jack started his new job as a J. Annie's store manager—three restless days before he'd know if he would be crushed by some secret, estrogen-based vocabulary, or if he could learn to properly fold a silk blouse, or even if he could stomach the smell of thirty eau de toilettes brawling with one another—Rebecca left him. Nothing personal, she insisted in the hand-scribbled note left unsubtly wedged between two lagers chilling in the fridge. It was time for her to move on, move out, move away.

Jack wanted to believe that he had nothing to do with her fast escape. He was sure she was right about it being nothing personal. He was glad, in fact, that the shrew had moved halfway across the country. She was a hot piece of ass—nothing more. He didn't necessarily want more, he just wanted better, nicer... and hornier.

Chapter Two

Awkward is how Jack would label his early days at J. Annie's—kind of a persistent discomfort that began during his interview. He sensed his initial meeting with Mike Allen, the chain-smoking, twitchy district manager for the southwest region, had not gone particularly well. Jack had had no strategy or plan in place to play up his somewhat dubious organizational and leadership qualities. He wasn't sure how relevant his sporting goods background might be to the women's wear business, and he wore that uncertainty quite visibly, like the greasy biscuit crumb clinging tight to the lapel of his navy blue suit.

If Jack had truly wanted the job, if he had tried really hard for it, he was sure he would have never gotten the offer. But, as Mike would explain four days later when they met at an uncomfortable, crowded coffee shop two blocks from the store, Jack's management and operational background was a perfect fit for their high volume business. The rest of the knowledge that Jack would need, the less important stuff like knowing what a hemline was, or that a dart was not always a pointy thing thrown in a bar, would be covered in training.

The meeting had wound down to aimless, perfunctory questions when Mike shoved a thick envelope across the small Formica two-top he'd enlisted as provisional office furniture. The weary table was large enough to accommodate two giant Styrofoam cups and a couple of cinnamon rolls, yet cozy enough to smoothly ferry Mike's coffee breath from one side to the other. Jack watched as the sealed packet rolled over a disorderly path of spilled sugar granules and headed his way.

Mike didn't say a word. He just pushed the envelope, like he was playing tabletop shuffleboard. Jack wasn't sure what was going on. Was he supposed to act excited at the unexpected, mysterious gift? Should he open it? He was pretty sure it wasn't something he was supposed to ignore, but Mike just sat there silent, his thin grin quivering a little at one end.

Jack looked away as if he hadn't noticed anything, such as a curious envelope, slide toward him. His drifting gaze found, and then locked, on a pair of spectacular tits, and the adorable, flexing barista they belonged to. He wasn't sure why she was arched in such a position. Her busy hands were hidden from Jack's view, but her soft, plump knockers were unmistakably visible, scarcely veiled by her low cut, snug blouse. He was certain if he stared long enough, one, or both, of her barely imprisoned orbs would spring free.

"That, my friend, will become commonplace scenery soon—a pen on a desk, if you will." Mike's words slapped at Jack's ears, and he turned quickly from the girl. "I trust you can handle it...professionally." Mike nudged the envelope a little closer to Jack, his right eyebrow vaulting as he leaned in. "Go ahead, open it. It's your employment agreement—nothing out of the ordinary. I think you'll do well at J. Annie's. I hope you accept."

Jack slipped a finger under the flap of the envelope and removed the contents. He scanned the agreement quickly, checking for worrisome keywords like *forever*, or *perpetuity*. Having no desire to blow the deal by questioning items a fourth grader would totally understand, and having made a cursory scan of the document without stumbling over one of his red-flag keywords, he nodded and folded the agreement back to its original state.

"There's something else in there." Mike spoke while slapping a pack of cigarettes against his palm, as if he were punishing the contents. "I took the liberty...well, just make sure it works for you."

Jack had noticed something else in the envelope, but assumed it was a duplicate copy of the agreement. It wasn't a copy. It was a travel itinerary, bundled with an air ticket to New York. The plane would leave Phoenix Sky Harbor airport in three days.

"Training. Two weeks training." Mike's empty hand reached across the table, the sleeve of his designer suit jacket overtaxed from the stretch. "When you return, you'll know everything you need to know."

Jack grabbed Mike's hand, not wanting to leave him hanging. But he did want to mull things over—at least for a minute or two. "I'm not sure what to say. This would all start in three days, huh?"

"Trust me," Mike answered, gesturing toward the busty barista. "I think you'll enjoy this more than peddling yoga mats."

M.L. Joslyn

***

There were two life lessons Jack would pluck from his training sessions at corporate. Two things that, as long as his mind was in some kind of working order, he would never forget.

First: don't ever accept a middle seat on a five-hour flight, even if a hot blonde with giant tits has the aisle seat. Her husband could be on the same flight, three rows back, and he may have promised his wife he'd watch their infant son until after takeoff—just after takeoff.

Second: being a buyer for a women's clothing company is one of the best gigs ever.

Jack was certain that Gerald Werle, the vice-president of operations, and perpetually pensive executive who had signed off on his trip expenses, would not be pleased to know that these were the nuggets his new hire had extracted from two weeks of costly, intensive training.

Regardless, these were the highlights of the trip for Jack—his enlightenment, so to speak. He would always remember that giant tits were sometimes there for a reason. And he would always aspire to hold Riley Duberman's job.

Part of Jack's two-week orientation at J. Annie's headquarters, a sprawling low-rise tucked securely onto a barbed wire infested corner of the Bronx, involved shadowing various corporate guys through their day. The intent of this exercise quickly became obvious to Jack: learn what these people do, understand what these people do, and never bother them again. In other words, get all the stupid questions out of the way now.

Riley Duberman barged into a small conference room one morning as Jack sat alone watching a mind-numbing video on merchandise processing. "You're mine for the day, buddy. Come."

Jack followed the slightly portly, more than slightly balding, energetic man from the room, trotting just to keep up. Riley remained silent during the quick walk to the parking lot, motioning to Jack when they had reached his car.

"So, you're the new Phoenix guy, huh?" Riley leaned into the steering wheel as he spoke, even though his seat was already positioned inches from the windshield. Jack had a terrifying vision of

10

an unanticipated airbag-deploying incident creating an atomic level explosion inside the car. "Having fun so far?"

"Sure." Jack had already learned to let the execs do all the talking.

"Good deal. We're taking a little trip into town, do a little buying—maybe."

"Maybe?"

"The price has to be right. Nobody can beat our prices, Jack. That means I can't pay as much as the next guy."

"Why would anyone want to sell to us then?"

"Because we can buy a shitload more pieces than the next guy. Sometimes I'll buy everything they've got."

"So, they love you then?"

"Love is not too strong a word, Jack. Not too strong."

Riley's black Lincoln rolled into Manhattan—Prince Bargain Hunter behind the wheel—his newly minted sidekick riding shotgun. They inched forward toward the garment district on 7th Avenue, hobbled by traffic that clotted like an artery strung out on Katz's pastrami. Riley flicked the windshield wiper lever anytime someone brandishing a paper towel and bottle of Windex came near.

"You're a good looking young man, Jack. I bet you work out a lot, probably eat healthy too. Thick brown hair, dark blue eyes, well dressed—single?"

"Recently." Jack found Riley's statement and question curious. He wrenched together his inner zoom lens and eyeballed the man from a fresh perspective.

"Make sure your store runs smoothly. Don't give the corporate guys any grief. And enjoy the hell out of this thing."

"I'll do my best." This you're-really-going-to-love-this-job crap was beginning to gnaw at Jack. It was a job. There would be women around. Big deal. He could make better sense of these dangled carrots if his job description included serving cocktails at a topless beach. But that wasn't the case. His job was to manage a couple dozen employees and sell as many clothes, or "shmatas," as everyone at corporate referred to them, as he could. Maybe they were just testing him, Jack thought. Maybe this was how they weeded out all the pervs.

Riley squeezed his bulky car through the narrow entrance of an ancient, smelly garage somewhere off 7th Avenue. He left the key in the ignition, grabbed a ticket from an attendant, and started walking—at a jogger's clip—from the garage.

"Here we are—Trend Ten Fashions. Do me a favor. Don't talk…unless someone asks you a question directly. Then, just say something funny. These guys all like to think they've got a sense of humor." Riley spoke without turning his head. Jack had fallen two paces behind.

Trend Ten Fashions stretched with a sophisticated, contemporary flair across the twenty-seventh floor of a well preserved, Art Deco building in the heart of New York's garment district. Hallways angled out from the expansive lobby in unexpected, non-symmetrical patterns. The deftly designed, modern space seemed a triumph over the heavy architectural elements of the building itself.

Riley and Jack emerged from a small, crowded elevator, just steps from the reception desk.

"Good morning, Mr. Duberman!" The slim woman with a tight sweater, full chest, and broad smile circled from behind a sizable, ebony counter. Her blue eyes lit like sparklers under a starless sky as she approached Riley, her seductive frame positioning for their embrace. A gentle, yet assertive amalgam of exotic spice and wildflowers arrived just before she did, and Jack breathed her in from arm's length. His prick twitched when her tits smashed shamelessly into Riley's softly padded chest.

"Tina, meet my friend Jack Timmons, one of our new store managers. I'm teaching him everything I know. It should take about five minutes."

Jack could tell Riley was in his element. It was like some sensor had activated another level of the man Jack had not yet seen. Jack discreetly covered his crotch, not wanting Riley to see the new level *he* was reaching.

"You are too funny, Riley Duberman!" Tina was still squeezing the big guy as she squealed-out the words.

"Alright, he's mine now Tina." A well-dressed, middle-aged man tapped Riley on the shoulder. "Follow me, men. I've got a great new line to show you."

Riley and Jack paced behind Ross Martin, their Trend Ten account exec, down one of the oddly oriented hallways toward a small, private showroom. After a few steps, Jack took a peek over his shoulder, just in case Tina had decided to lift her sweater to do some unwarranted primping. He didn't consider it a hopeful waste of time, but a distinct possibility.

With introductions out of the way, the men settled around a short rectangular table at one end of the boxy, well-lit room. Jack wondered silently where all the clothes were stashed.

Two minutes into an unseasonable debate over whether the Yankees needed to raid the free agent market yet again, the spring-hinged door to the room pressed open. In walked two of the prettiest, leggiest, most alluring girls Jack could recall seeing. They were twins from the neck down, and cream-inducing fashion models from the toes up.

The girls, Crystal and Alyssa, were clothed in coordinating brief skirts and sheer blouses that differed only in color; Crystal's, a pale peach, just a degree or two from pink—Alyssa's, a soft blue that Jack determined right there and then to be the color of heaven.

They each kept a hand on a hip, fingers splayed, just like a good model should. They remained shadow quiet, yet they screamed seduction. Their smiles were brighter than hundred watt bulbs, their shoulder-length wavy hair impossibly lustrous.

Jack made a quick, discreet assessment of the amazingly perky, generous handfuls that floated like fishing bobbers beneath the thin fabric of their sleeveless tops. His cock began to unwind as Crystal and Alyssa circled the table, allowing everyone to have a good look, ostensibly at the freshly available fashions. Jack made sure he was not cheated.

While the girls frolicked about the small space, touching Riley's shoulder here, caressing Jack's arm there, the door to the room creaked opened. In walked a beautiful figurine of a woman, a woman that for some indefinable reason Jack determined to be of questionable sexual orientation. He could easily spy teacup breasts and stiff nipples beneath her flimsy, silky blouse. His cock raised full from the torrent of fleshly delights, the tip knocking at the waistband of his boxers.

The woman held the door open with a sandaled foot while pulling a chrome-plated rolling rack into the room. The rack was tight with assorted, pastel-shaded clothing draped, hung, or clipped onto polished, wooden hangers.

"Gentlemen, may I present our new line of signature casual." Ross gestured with one arm, as if he were Ed Sullivan introducing The Beatles for the first time.

The figurine smiled then ambled from the room, the jiggling silhouette of her small, firm breasts drawing the group's attention. Crystal and Alyssa licked their lips, and Jack wondered if it was a subliminal come-on of sorts, or a totally unrestrained display of sentiment. The rack of clothes remained against the far wall, two paces from the table.

Ross nodded toward the models, his thin lips snaking into a calculated smirk and rising at the corners; Jack considered the man might possess some genetic connection to the Grinch.

The girls seemed to have no problem deciphering their boss's tacit instructions. Crystal reached for a cluster of hangers and handed half to Alyssa. They moved to opposite ends of the rack, pulled thin, chrome extension bars from cleverly concealed hiding places, and then placed the hangers onto the empty extensions. With practiced efficiency they relieved themselves of their overworked outfits and exchanged them for fresh pieces.

Riley extracted a small notepad from the inside pocket of his jacket and began jotting furiously. He was a professional, and he had a job to do. Crystal, Alyssa, and Ross were doing their thing as well, albeit with a brothel-keeper/working girl twist. Jack had a different notion, making it his business to leer at the unblushing, beautiful girls as they hustled to remove their blouses.

Jack had always considered himself more of a leg and ass man than a breast man—not that anyone had ever asked. But Crystal and Alyssa weren't shy about letting their girls grab some face time with the clients, and Jack wasn't about to let his senseless order of preference interfere with a good time. In fact, the longer he ogled the full, smooth globes dancing and bobbing just out of reach, the less he cared about silly proclivities.

"Okay, now we'll be moving on to the "S" series, starting with our S300 tops and bottoms." Ross began speaking a little more like a businessman and a little less like P.T. Barnum as the meeting progressed.

As the models pulled their fifth set of outfits from the rack, Jack noted a curious trend in their behavior. They had no problem removing their tops in front of the trio of men, whirling their goods about like drunken cowboys with unholstered pistols. However, when it came to slipping out of their skirts and shorts, they'd turn away from the table in some incongruous homage to modesty. They continued to face away from the men as they stepped into the fresh pieces.

Jack couldn't follow their reasoning. It wasn't as if the girls were hiding much, or anything really, with their pointless about-face. They had on underwear—kind of. More specifically, they wore matching light blue thongs constructed with the same amount of material as found in a finger puppet. Jack became occupied with this conundrum to the point where it became his reason for being in the room; he finally had a purpose, a job to do. Why had Crystal and Alyssa been so brazen and shameless about everything else? Was there some kind of New York state law that precluded them from full frontal semi-nudity? Was it part of the sales pitch? Was it possible they possessed a grain of bashfulness?

The irony of it all was that as the girls bent to step out of their skirts and shorts, Jack was offered perhaps a better show than if they had been facing him. Of all the material in the tiny thongs, over ninety percent had gone toward fabricating the narrow, slit-covering triangle up front; another eight percent toward the tinier triangle in back that hovered just above their ass cracks. The remaining two percent—a narrow ribbon around the waist and one linking the two triangles—held the whole thing together.

Crystal and Alyssa's perfectly tight butts bubbled in the direction of the table, and, as they flexed, reached, or leaned over, the obscured, thin strip of ribbon that tied the front of their panties to the back would appear—a powder blue warning sign—more conspicuous than a beacon in a lighthouse. The ribbon hid little, yet somehow maintained a calculated, frustratingly accurate path along the girl's most intimate openings.

The rest was there for all to see, however fleeting the glimpse: bikini-waxed knobs of supple flesh straddling tight slits—pale skin shading darker and puckering as it nudged backdoors. Framing these distractions were the most delectable asses—mouthwatering, well-defined, resilient spheres of weighty nourishment.

The men at the table, two of them occupied with actual work, were treated to quite a sight. Jack wished he could survey all that the ribbons had covered, edged against, and alluded to. But he couldn't deny the erotic power of the scaled down lingerie. He would be dreaming of pale blue ribbons forever.

"What do you think, Jack?" Riley seemed sincerely interested in the younger man's opinion.

"A-maz-ing." Jack mumbled the word in spurts, swallowing between syllables. He had been caught dreaming, or fantasizing, or maybe just staring—he wasn't sure. He didn't want to look down, but his dick had been begging for more room and he could only imagine the spectacle on parade. He wished Riley and Ross would trot off to sign paperwork somewhere.

"Okay, then..." Ross fumbled with some forms, his eyes locked to Riley's. "I can do the line at thirty off—if I can get your usual commitment."

Riley and Ross's voices slid to a whirring buzz of background noise. Jack's gaze steadied on the girls, who were busy placing their modeled outfits back on the rolling rack. Crystal noticed Jack leering, and smiled.

Alyssa grabbed one end of the rack, waiting for her partner to grab the other end. Crystal held one finger up, signaling "just a minute," and then sauntered over to Jack.

Jack's eyes shifted toward the real businessmen in the room, confirming they were otherwise occupied. Crystal leaned in to Jack's ear, her shoulder-length locks teasing his neck. Her left hand glided gently over his trousers, pacing off the reach of his stiff root.

"It's good when we turn from you, no?" Crystal whispered with minty breath and a foreign accent. Jack guessed she was from a place ending in ia, like Yugoslavia, or Russia maybe. Then, he remembered that heaven wasn't spelled that way.

Chapter Three

"They're ready for you, Jack," Julie announced through the yawning door of the manager's office. "Morning meeting time!"

Jack leaned back in his overstuffed desk chair, hands laced behind his head. What the hell would he talk about today, he wondered. Corporate had demanded continuous communication between managers and store associates, which meant daily meetings—warranted or not. Mike Allen, Jack's DM, likened these summits to a company newsletter without the paper or irrelevant, morality-charged cartoons. Jack had always thought that this method of interfacing with employees was an okay idea, but after a year of standing before them, morning after morning, he'd run out of interesting, or even entertaining, things to say.

All fourteen of the morning shift associates mingled in cliques of twos and threes in front of the broad checkout counter, yapping, giggling, and commiserating. Jack ambled toward them, holding tight to a marked-up, wounded clipboard. He brought this prop to every meeting, thinking it made him look like he had some sort of agenda.

"Ahem! Excuse me everyone! Let's get started." Jack watched his employees fall into a single line in front of the checkout counter. Most of them leaned against the waist high fixture. A few of the younger ones used it as a seat. Jack didn't mind. He never intended for these meetings to last more than a few minutes. Sometimes he'd get carried away though, usually over something inane, like why tampons should never be stocked in the break room snack machine, and the meeting would go on and on. He often wished he could sit on the counter, too.

As the group settled in, Jack took his usual position across from them, about four feet from the counter; he didn't want to have to speak too loud and waste his voice. He contemplated the day's lineup of J. Annie's associates, making sure he had all posts covered. Stockroom staff—check. Fitting room staff—check. Cashiers—check. Supervisory personnel so he could hang out and do nothing all day—check.

Julie situated herself at one end of the row, pen and pad in hand in case Jack said something important. It amazed him how many notes she would take at these meetings. He had never said anything important. Sometimes, he'd feel bad about all the made up crap he'd babble on and on about—but he always enjoyed watching Julie write it all down.

At the other end of the row, his stock supervisor, Joel, stood by himself, separated from the girls by a few feet, as if cooties were a real disease.

Filling the space between Julie and Joel, the rest of the staff bided their time, lingering in a resigned posture, waiting for Jack to start his blathering presentation. The group of mostly twenty-somethings, with a couple of thirty-somethings and teens thrown in for balance, were doing their best to appear at least somewhat attentive; typically, they'd be able to sustain this charade for about three minutes.

Perched comfortably on the counter directly in front of Jack, his youngest employee, Sarah Bartholomew, prepared herself for the meeting. The composed eighteen-year-old pressed her palms flat against the counter's surface, bracing for a potential sermon. She flaunted impish, flickering green eyes, and a very short red plaid skirt, that seemed to shorten even further as she sat. Every few seconds she would drive her long, blonde curls from her face with an almost neurotic swish of her head. Jack had hired her in spite of, or more likely because of the fact that the only "job" listed on her resume was as a Head Cheerleader while a senior in high school.

"Mr. Timmons?" Sarah breathed his name, yet her voice somehow carried well. "Are we going to talk about when we can take our vacation time? There's a concert in L.A. next week I really, really want to go to."

"No, Sarah. Talk to Julie after the meeting. She'll see what she can do." Jack glanced quickly at his cute assistant manager who was busy scribbling this significant nugget on her pad. "In today's meeting, Sarah, we're going to discuss how to get our shipments processed and out to the sales floor quicker."

As Jack began his lecture about why merchandise buried in the stock room probably doesn't sell very well, Sarah decided to make known her displeasure at her boss's fucked up sense of priorities.

Stretching back, she laid her head on the counter with a soft plunk. She emitted a loud sigh as she stared wide-eyed at the ceiling, committed to ignoring her manager's directives. She persisted with this tantrum, whimpering quiet, yet still perceptible, *hmmpfs*.

Of course, Jack's attention was drawn to the petulant part-timer, who remained parked with her back pressed against the hard work surface. It seemed to him a sleight-of-hand trick the way her red plaid skirt continued to recede as he spoke; it had risen so high that it was barely shielding the top of her thighs. She was a pouting, immature girl, but she suddenly appeared to Jack as a calculating siren who knew what she was doing. She possessed some outstanding assets, and she was going to use them to get her way.

Jack didn't want to look, but he couldn't help it; the girl was just a few feet away, directly in front of him. Her shiny, black, Mary Janes dangled above the floor, wriggling like a worm on a hook. Jack took the bait, his eyes fixed on the unanticipated, curiously arousing display.

Sarah's mesmerizing, dancing toes captured Jack's gaze. He had found his starting place—his brick one of the yellow road. Beginning with the tips of her shoes, he traced a pair of white Kate Spade knee-highs as they rose provocatively up her legs. Jack knew the brand, as they were an item stocked in his store—third spinner from the accessory counter, top row. They hugged Sarah's firm calves exactly as they should. He knew that too, as he'd analyzed the full-color photograph of the leggy model on the packaging more than once—or maybe more than a few dozen times.

The top of the socks pinched at Sarah's well-defined cheerleader limbs just slightly—enough to encourage further exploration up the compelling, nicely muscled road. Her legs rested flat against the counter and spilled out a little, but not in an unappealing, overly fleshy way. Their orientation only enhanced the lean athleticism of the girl's sinewy thighs.

Jack continued to speak, his ordinary mind working hard to stay engaged. This was not an easy accomplishment. There were two quite disparate threads toying with his concentration: staying on task to convey the importance of an empty stockroom, and staying on top of the sexy eighteen year old who refused to sit up and pay attention. Jack was a musician on stage, trying to finger pick an instrument and

M.L. Joslyn

sing at the same time; he didn't think he'd be able to maintain this taxing level of coordination for long.

Jack hadn't allowed his eyes to point where they were desperate to point—not yet. But he knew if he didn't sneak a look soon, he might miss the most significant event of his day, or week, or however long it would take to supplant the anticipated, breathtaking image. He finally caved, allowing his gaze to bathe in the warmth of Sarah's firm, creamy thighs. His vision then swept toward the spot in between—the warm, seductive, slim space that he could no longer dodge.

It was there, just as Jack had imagined—just as he had hoped. Balanced in the gap was a narrow sheath of chaste-white fabric that covered her thin slit, or rolling gash, or whatever it was that remained hidden by the small swath of cloth. He was just glad that there was something there beyond an exposed beaver smiling back at him. If Sarah weren't wearing underwear, he would have been forced to look quickly away—or label himself some level of pervert.

He then realized that he *was* some grade of degenerate, staring at his part-time employee's crotch like this. He was already there though, and he decided he would soak up what he could before he had to let go.

Her pussy, or at least the part of it that had escaped from her snug, scant panties, was shaved; it seemed a ripe nectarine, choked by a length of rope. The cloaked essence of her anatomy was a simple mystery, easily solved. The white fabric had done its best to conceal what it could, given its limited span. But the warm, humid cotton had left a flawless impression, a perfect mold, a gift of sorts, for Jack to admire. He immersed himself in the landscape of peaks and valleys, and in the steadfast creek that ran north and south through it all.

Jack pulled back for one last look at the package: the red plaid skirt riding high above smooth, powerful thighs, the dangling legs wrapped in tall, white socks, the shiny black shoes slow dancing with the front of the counter—and the precious, thin, restricted area, that he would never, or should ever, lay eyes on again.

His employees had been oblivious, or so he guessed, to the almost fatal distraction that still sulked on the counter like a stubborn two-year-old. They had noticed her, of course, but he didn't think

20

they had noticed him noticing her. They leaned against the checkout counter—the whole line of them—pretending to listen, wanting to leave.

"Alright, that's enough for today, okay? Take ten before the store opens." Jack scanned the group for any sign that he may have breached their faith, or had maybe caused some awkward, hard to explain, emotional trauma. He saw only faces preoccupied with more important matters, like, how long the lines would be at the clubs that night.

"Julie, Cherry, could I see you in my office for a minute?" Jack stopped his assistant manager and store supervisor from shuffling with the rest of the herd to the break room.

After settling in behind his desk, Jack waited for the door to his cramped office to creak shut. Julie and Cherry stood stone straight in front of the desk, a questioning, uneasy cloud of confusion fogging their faces.

"You can sit down, ladies. You're not in trouble. Relax." Jack enjoyed the sight of the two girls pressed against his desk, their skinny slacks accentuating those sweet little triangles below their belts. But this wasn't the time for the splendid visual of Julie's slinky frame or Cherry's perpetual camel toe. Those treats were too much for him to handle just now, considering what he needed to discuss. "We need to talk about Sarah."

"I know!" Cherry interrupted. "She was such a baby at the meeting!"

"She's a teenager, Cherry," Julie said, in her typically sensible, mature tone. "She was just pouting. We probably shouldn't make a big deal about it, at least not right now. I'll see if I can give her the time off she wants."

"Thanks Julie, but that's not what I wanted to talk to you two about. It's her choice of work outfits. She needs to wear something...more." Jack looked down at his desk and began to shuffle some papers around.

"So..." Cherry let the word hang on her lips for a bit. It drove Jack crazy that she would start every sentence this way. One day he hoped she would learn to formulate her thoughts before speaking. "She bought that outfit here. We're allowed to wear anything we want, if it's something we sell."

M.L. Joslyn

"I'm familiar with that policy," Jack replied. "But, we can't take everything too literally, right? We sell bathing suits, but I think we'd all agree they wouldn't make for a proper work outfit."

"So, what exactly is the problem with what she's wearing?" Julie asked. Cherry nodded, approving of the question.

"Well, her skirt's a little bit skimpy, wouldn't you say? I mean, when she laid back on the checkout counter, I couldn't help but see all the way to Mars."

"Are you sure you don't mean the moon?" Cherry thought she was being clever. Both girls chuckled.

"Jack, if it makes you feel better, I'm sure she doesn't consider you a degenerate creep or anything. I'm guessing she caught you taking a good look?"

"No, Julie, she didn't catch me taking a…whatever. I would just like both of you to convey to Sarah, and the rest of the staff, that they need to be reasonable about what they wear to work. If they show up in a micro-skirt, I'll have to send them home."

"Or spank them?" Cherry smiled as she spoke. "I actually think her skirt is cute. I was considering buying one. Do I get a spanking too?"

Jack could sense he was losing control of the meeting. He could also sense a pint of blood flooding his face.

"You know, Jack," Julie said in her serious tenor, "It wouldn't be anything new to Sarah if she caught you, or any guy, looking up her skirt. She was a cheerleader. She's used to it."

"I wasn't, I mean I didn't want to…"

"Mr. Timmons? Can I come in?"

"I'm kind of in the middle of a meeting, Carrie. And, could you please knock before barging in next time?" Jack didn't want to come across like he was pissed at one of his best sales associates. He was grateful, in fact, for her unmannerly interruption.

"But, it's Evi Jansen. She wants your opinion on a blouse. Actually, she doesn't want your opinion. She insists. According to her, *Zhock Teemanss hass zee best taste in zee vimohn's close.* Please? I could use the sale."

"Oh boy. Okay. Where is she? And is she…decent?" Jack was all too familiar with Evi. She regularly sought his male perspective on fashion—tight fitting, low-cut fashion. As the manager of a women's

22

wear store, he could never consider her requests out of line. After all, he was supposed to be an arbiter of style. He kind of enjoyed how the girls who shopped in his store assumed he knew what the fuck he was talking about. But there was something about Evi. She was a hot, fortyish woman with a huge set of knockers and a Scandinavian accent that Jack found both disquieting and disarming. Almost tauntingly, she sported an enormous diamond on her delicate ring finger. It sparkled like a disco ball when she flapped her hand about.

And then, there was this peculiar behavior of hers that always made him uncomfortable, always gave him pause: Evi would never look Jack in the eye during their conversations. It wasn't that she was shy, or introverted in any way—it's that she was busy looking elsewhere. It was a bizarre, non-verbal game they would play whenever they had an exchange. Jack would stare at her pale blue eyes in an attempt to make a sincere connection. Evi would stare at his pants zipper in an attempt to discern a thickening prick. Was her ego that needy? Did she have to be regularly assured that her assets could still charm a snake? Would the man that placed the giant diamond on her finger show up one day, spy Jack's physical response to his wife's bumper crop, and beat the crap out of him? Jack enjoyed Evi, but carefully, warily.

"Cherry, Julie, you guys stay in my office. We're not done. And, if I'm not back in a few minutes, page me, okay?" Jack closed the office door behind him and took a deep breath.

"Zhock! Sank you for seeing me. Now, be honest! Am I too olt for zees blouse?" Evi screeched at Jack as she ran up to him outside his office.

"Too old? What sort of question is that, Evi? You're a beautiful young lady!" Jack wanted to avoid glancing at the blouse, kind of like a kid wanted to ignore a giant bag of Halloween candy.

"You are too sveet, Zhock! Ant too funny! Now, look ant tell me."

"Well, Evi, I'd say this blouse was designed specifically with you in mind." Jack had no choice but to look at the blouse now, even though Evi wasn't tracking his eyes. It wasn't so much the blouse that he noticed at first, but the cleavage. Her pillowy tits might have been less obvious if she'd tried on a more properly fitted size six instead of a two, had worn a bra, and had buttoned the top three buttons as the designer intended. As it was, her jiggling orbs appeared to be fighting for escape, her prominent nipples punching heroically through the thin material.

Jack couldn't help it. His cock was thinking for itself, whistling its own tune. It uncoiled with a steady determination and pressed against his trousers, asserting its power. There was little Jack could do about it. Evi had edged closer to him, leaving just a small gap between her tits and his chest—a wide enough space for her to scrutinize the commotion in his pants—the perfect distance for Jack to best enjoy her wonderful spread.

"You are right, Zhock! It vas mate for me. I'll take it!" Evi bumped up against Jack and gave him a little smooch before prancing back to the fitting room. Her personal penile barometer had said yes to the blouse, and she was pleased.

Although Jack was left hanging, he managed to shuffle discreetly back to his office, easing along a strategic, unpopulated path. He pressed open the door to see Julie and Cherry inches from each other, sharing whispers. They appeared nonplussed, as if they hadn't expected him to return.

"How'd it go?" Julie asked.

"The usual," Jack replied, scurrying to take a seat behind his desk.

"She gave you a good look at those melons of hers, huh?" Cherry asked. "I swear she only shops here because of our community fitting rooms. I'm surprised she hasn't killed anyone with those cans, the way she parades them around."

"Listen, let's finish our conversation about the store dress code." Jack wanted to talk about anything other than Evi's huge, luscious tits. He still had a semi, which, if the girls didn't let up about the woman, could go either way.

"Did she vant to eat you, Zhock? Maybe let you fondle her tulips?" Cherry asked the questions with a straight face. Julie burst out laughing.

"Girls! Cut it out! This stuff isn't easy for me to deal with. You both know that."

"You know what I think? Cherry shifted in her chair to address Julie. "I think Jack's been single for too long. He needs to get... you know."

"Alright," Jack said, eyes rolling," I want both of you to convey to the staff the importance of proper attire. I really don't want to have to talk about this again. Oh, and while you have their attention, remind them to keep the fitting room curtain secured. Now go. I've got work to do, and so do you."

"Wait," Cherry said. "Would it be okay if I opened tomorrow instead of working the closing shift? I've got some things I need to take care of."

"I'll switch with you, Cherry," Julie said. "I don't mind closing tomorrow."

"You're a sweetie, Julie. Thanks."

"No problem, sugar. You've helped me out plenty of times."

"Okay, lovebirds," Jack said. "Why don't the two of you go find a perch out on the sales floor? Let me get back to work—please?"

Jack watched Julie and Cherry stretch their hands to the ceiling and then step from his office.

As soon as the word *lovebirds* had left his lips, he'd regretted it. Now he couldn't shake the image: Julie and Cherry—naked—fondling each other's tits and going at each other's dimpled nests like woodpeckers drumming on cedar. He'd had fantasies about each of them, but they had always starred either Julie, or, if he were feeling particularly depraved, Cherry.

Jack peeked from his office window just in time. The girls were headed across the sales floor together, their juicy butts seesawing inside their snug pants. After a minute, they were gone from sight—but not from Jack's dreams.

Chapter Four

"Good morning ladies!" Jack spun his key to unlock the metal-framed, cartoonishly tall double doors that flashed J. Annie's whimsical logo. After allowing his trusted morning prep crew, Emily and Trish, to enter, he scurried to turn off the store's alarm.

Jack planted himself behind his desk, booted-up his computer, and watched his email quickly fill the screen. There was the usual string of missives from corporate: shipment notifications, merchandise alerts, prescriptive memos. He printed them all and then sorted through them. He plucked the most urgent ones, the ones he had to deal with himself, from the stack.

As Jack leafed through the papers, someone tapped on his office door—lightly—but purposefully. He was sure it was Cherry; it was all the sound she could screw up with those girlishly slight hands of hers. Without waiting for a response, the twenty-year-old store supervisor worked the door open and positioned herself against her boss's desk. Her small frame, full tits, and radiant, luminous, and foreboding beam of a smile floated like a peppermint cloud above him.

"Hi Jack! I saw Emily and Trish headed toward the stock room. Thought I'd poke my head in the door—see what's up."

"Just doing some paperwork. You seem to be in a good mood this morning." Cherry had jettisoned a rush of sweet and fresh scents when she'd made her whirling entrance; the stirring aroma was pummeling Jack in all the right places. He grabbed the opportunity to eye his store supervisor, whose thighs were pressed firmly against his desk.

"I'm always in a good mood—you know that. So, I had a couple questions I wanted to ask, if you've got a minute."

"Sure. Say, before I forget, I got another security memo today. I swear, one bad inventory and corporate thinks we've forgotten how to lock the doors at night. We're a top ten store in sales and quality care surveys, but I guess that's meaningless. Anyway, do you have some time today to spend up in the perch, behind the two-way?"

"Seriously, Jack? That's like the most tedious waste of time job in the world. Here's the deal: when I'm old enough to take up knitting, I'll sit up there all day. Until then, I've got lots better things to keep my eyes on, like the sales floor and the fitting rooms. Besides, if we've got little thieves running around, I can see them much better at ground level. Why don't you send Joel up there?"

"Well, he wouldn't be able to do his stock work then, would he? Besides, someone from management needs to sign off on it. It's okay. I'll ask Julie. Or, I'll just do it myself. What was it you wanted to ask, anyway?"

"So, this is kind of personal..."

Cherry's eyes danced about as she strained to cobble together her question. Jack continued to breathe her in, literally, and visually. He loved the way her wavy, auburn hair would bounce about her face when she moved even just a little. Sometimes a tress would sweep down into her eyes and she would brush it away with an innocent sensuality, almost as if she were promising to play with it later, alone.

"I wanted to ask you about Rebecca, your ex..."

Jack glanced at Cherry's thighs, wondering why the girl continued to lean against the hard edge of his desk. He figured if she held them like that much longer, she'd have to take an iron to them. Not that she was fragile or insubstantial. She was a wisp of a thing, really. But she wasn't like other wispy girls. Jack had never really considered her small, at least not by conventional standards. Along with her outsized personality, Cherry possessed a set of serious, outsized breasts that pretty much negated any tininess about her. They seemed to hover rather than hang. They were the kind of boobs other women would pretend not to notice while thinking: *someday, when I have the money...* But Cherry's tits were real—just like her bright smile, and oft-times discomfiting plain-spokenness.

"So, was she fun at all? I mean, did you break up because she was a bore?"

Before Jack learned to appreciate Cherry for who she was—back when he was getting his feet wet in the business—he only thought of her as that girl who loved to show off her pussy. It wasn't hard for him to remember her name. Cherry—the pussy girl. The way her slacks molded to her body was so intoxicating, she was basically half a person to him—a from the waist down person. And she always wore them too, those slacks of hers; not the same pair over and over, but the same fit over and over. They weren't all tight, at least not in the leg. Still, they all seemed to fall through the cracks, so to speak. Jack couldn't imagine Cherry ever being comfortable, what with her cootch covered tighter than a brand new jar of pickles. But if she were bothered at all by the constricting bottoms that were her trademark, she never let it show; and she wasn't the type to keep things curtained.

"Why would you want to know if she was a bore? Why would you want to know anything about her? Where did this come from?" Jack asked, his eyes finally meeting up with hers.

"I guess I'm trying to understand you better, that's all. We've worked together for a year, and I don't really know you yet. You know?"

"No, I don't know," Jack answered. "We work together. I thought we understood each other pretty well."

"Yeah, we do. But, you seem like an interesting guy. I'd like to know more about that guy—that's all. I'm sorry. I guess I'm just too nosy sometimes."

Jack realized that Cherry was hitting on him—maybe. But, why else would she be asking about his ex-girlfriend? He hated these games.

"Listen," Jack started, "Rebecca was not a boring girl at all. She was more crazy than boring, if there were a scale for such things. Maybe, at the end of our relationship, she was a bit...lifeless, I suppose. But that's not why we broke up. Okay?"

"Okay. I just wondered about her. That's all."

"Fine. It's time to open the store, Cherry. Do you want to take care of that, please?"

Cherry pushed off from Jack's desk, her bright smile undimmed from their conversation. Jack sensed warm air thinning to cool as Cherry edged away from him, and toward his office door. He exhaled with a sigh as it began to close behind her.

"Oh, by the way Jack," Cherry said, leaning back into his office, "I can be crazy too. And I promise you, I'm never lifeless." With a wink and a wave, she allowed the door to click shut.

Jack could hear fading splintery sounds—a moist, drawn-out kiss he thought—just outside his office. He wasn't sure how he would handle this. Cherry was definitely coming on to him; even slow-on-the-uptake Jack could see that. This was a problem. But it was only a problem because he wanted her. He'd wanted her for a long while. He knew if he fucked up this opportunity he'd be kicking himself for years.

What he really wanted was to get down between her legs, lick off the paint she called pants, and suck on her full, juicy twat. He already had a pretty good idea of what it looked like; he could only imagine what it tasted like. It was a hot, glazed donut sitting in the bakery window, and he was the boy on the other side of the glass, staring, drooling. Now the window was open, and he was yearning for a mouthful of the sweet, fresh pastry.

Jack was very clear on company policy: don't dip your pen in company ink, or your bucket in the company well, or some such crap. But there was also the issue of Cherry being ten years younger than him. Did it matter? No, he decided quickly. She came on to him. She didn't have a problem with his age, so why should he? Was he some sort of lecherous old man? Maybe. Did he like having a twenty-year-old hitting on him? Definitely.

This was the opportunity, the foot in the door Jack had been hoping for. But this gift he'd been given, this loosely wrapped present, forced him to evaluate his shallowness, his selfishness. If it were Julie that had made these brash overtures toward him, he would have been just as happy. He started thinking about the other girls on his staff. Would he turn any of them down, he wondered? He still had the respect of his employees; at least he assumed he did. He knew if he started fucking one of their coworkers, word would spread quickly, and that respect would disappear faster than a pint of Ben & Jerry's in the break room.

With a full workday ahead, Jack made the executive decision to shelve the matter of Cherry and her come-on, at least temporarily. He shuffled through the pile of memos he had printed earlier looking for something to do, something to help take his mind off things. Someone had to spend an hour in the security perch. If there were a better way to waste a few brain cells while staying sober, it wasn't coming to him.

The security perch was a throwback to when the retail industry relied on people to run the business—before sophisticated anti-theft hardware and security cameras made humans more useless than they already were.

The room itself was a simple, light deprived square space about the size of a small coat closet. A thick covering of black paint on three of its four walls kept the room dismal and ill defined. The fourth wall wasn't a wall at all, but a floor to ceiling two-way mirror. From the inside of the perch the view was similar to peering from a giant sunglass lens. From a shopper's perspective, the reflective glass appeared to be a design faux pas, an awkwardly placed mirror too high up the wall for practical use.

The room was secreted behind a nondescript door at one end of the sales floor, and was reached by climbing a narrow, metal staircase. The only furnishings it contained, or could even accommodate, were a small, metal folding chair, a paging microphone, and, if they hadn't been ironically stolen, a pair of binoculars.

Jack signaled to Cherry, who was standing outside one of the fitting room doors, that he was headed up to the perch. She waved back—her sparkling smile and hopeful eyes visible from the moon.

After a few minutes in the perch, and after a brief battle with the disagreeable, groaning, metal chair, Jack settled in for an hour of company mandated surveillance duty.

The store had been slowly filling with customers since Cherry had unlocked the front doors. Jack surveyed the small clusters of eager-to-spend young ladies that had filed through the entrance and then had fanned out, like well-armed hunters on a quest.

He kept a sharp eye on the few customers that seemed less focused, less intense. His training had taught him that they were either curious first-timers, or thieves, intentionally diverting attention from themselves by acting oblivious and dispassionate. This was a common ruse employed by these thorns in Jack's ass. Once they'd stuffed their purses and baggy slacks with merchandise, they'd sell it online, usually just hours later. Jack scooted the folding chair closer to the glass, determined to catch someone, should they be so bold.

Of course, he'd never caught anyone—ever. His stores were hit regularly, which was no revelation to him. It was a fact of retailing, a tradition as permanent, and invisible, as drunk driving. There had always been a small percentage of people who would leave his store with stuff they hadn't paid for. Most of them were good. They knew what they were doing. Jack was pretty sure he'd never catch any of these bandits. But he would never stop trying.

As the shoppers filtered toward the back of the store, closer to Jack, his interest in their behavior was piqued. These were the people he could see with detail. If their purses were open, he could spy into them from his lofted location and check for pilfered sunglasses or earrings. If they had failed to button the top couple buttons of their blouses, well, he could check the contents there, too, even though that sort of surreptitious behavior made him uncomfortable. Jack thought it unfair, not to mention a little perverted, for him to be furtively ogling unsuspecting women. If he were on the sales floor face-to-face, or face-to-ass, or face-to-tits with one of his customers, then it was game on. Usually, at least in Jack's mind, they wanted him to look. They loved flaunting their figures. He figured all girls had a little Evi in them; typically just a little more muffled, a little less brazen. But, when Jack was in the perch, they had no idea he was looking. He likened peering at inadvertently exposed cleavage to stealing. If his shoppers weren't supposed to steal clothes, he wasn't supposed to be stealing looks. Jack considered it inappropriate behavior, or at least a little creepy.

With this principled and virtuous game plan in his back pocket, Jack wriggled himself into a semi-comfortable position and locked his fingers behind his head. He let his eyes wander across the sales floor below, where a blonde girl wearing an insufficiently proportioned pair of denim shorts and loose fitting t-shirt caught his attention. From his angle she looked amazing, although he couldn't imagine her being less hot from any point of view. Her straight-as-a-country-road golden hair hid much of her face, but if the tip of her nose, full lips, and flawless complexion were any indication, she was a real babe.

This girl seemed very intent on shopping for just the right clothes. Jack would have been happy to stare at the beauty all day, but her behavior didn't jibe with his criteria for a typical shoplifter, and he had work to do.

Jack continued to scan the sales floor looking for unusual behavior, hoping in his gut that he wouldn't find any.

Peppered among the shoppers were several of Jack's employees, each busy with a customer, or, in Joel's case, with a rolling rack of fresh merchandise. Watching his staff at work was a great side benefit to hanging out in the security perch. It was a perfect set-up for him to discreetly assess his employee's productivity. Generally, he was very proud of their work habits, as if his fine leadership skills had something to do with their quality performance.

Occasionally, he'd spy a couple of his staff anchored against one of the walls, chatting, like they were on a cigarette break without the smoke. He'd only hassle them about their negligence if they pushed the limit, not that he had ever bothered to establish any such thing. Jack wanted his staff to enjoy their workdays. He understood that happy employees usually made for better employees.

The pretty blonde girl caught Jack's eye once again, this time just below his perch. She pawed through one of three round racks that were tight with clearance merchandise—mostly summer shorts and gauzy blouses—then selected a blouse and held it at arm's length. Jack couldn't tell if she were contemplating whether she liked the piece, or deciding whether it was pretty enough to make her girlfriends jealous.

Jack was about to drag his eyes away from the attractive blonde again so he could redirect his detective-keen mind on more suspicious types, when he noticed her looking around nervously, her head jerking right and left as if she were taking punches. She seemed to be scanning for something, or someone.

This was what Jack had climbed the metal steps for, and what he had hoped to never deal with. The hot blonde was going to attempt to swipe the blouse, and he was going to have to bust her.

He couldn't take his eyes off the girl. If he failed to witness the crime—her sleight of hand move—he would not be able to confront her. He didn't want to watch her steal the blouse, but he had to.

Blondie got herself into a crouch, low enough for her head, and just her head, to be exposed above the rail of the rack. She looked around making sure nobody could see her. She forgot to look up.

Jack wiped his sweaty palms on his pants and reached for the paging microphone. If this heist were going down, he'd need a partner—someone to keep their eyes on the girl while he hustled to make the collar. It had to be Cherry. He'd page her to the perch, explain things to her, and then send her back to the floor with instructions to glue her gaze to the girl.

There was always the possibility that the blonde could ditch the blouse in the time it took Jack to reach her. That's why he needed another set of eyes. He wouldn't risk a lawsuit. There could not be a moment when the girl wasn't being watched. Jack wasn't sure if he wanted to throw up now to get it out of his system, or wait until he had the girl in tears.

His fingers danced over the talk button on the paging microphone as he stared hard at the blonde, who was scrunched down just below the two-way mirror. He waited patiently for her to stuff the blouse into her purse. But, instead of secreting it away, she set it atop a nearby rack. She looked around briefly, and then peeled off the blouse she was wearing, exposing a surprisingly juicy set of jiggly handfuls. She then reached for the blouse she had set aside and pulled it over her head. Jack assumed she was switching blouses, a common practice of shoplifters that wanted to freshen their wardrobe—for free.

Jack waited for Blondie to ditch the old blouse under a rack and head for the exit, but she didn't seem to be in a hurry. Instead, with her old blouse in one hand, she began to scour through a different rack, one packed with sale shorts. She extracted three pairs, maneuvered over to her accustomed spot below Jack, and stripped off her shorts.

Jack's palms were still sweaty, but for a different reason now. The golden-haired babe, a natural blonde for certain, was nude from the waist down. The intoxicating show progressed from soft-core frontal to hard-core yawning as she shifted to one knee while unclipping the three pairs of shorts from their hangers.

Jack couldn't believe his luck. This girl wasn't stealing. She was trying on clothes. What he didn't understand was, why here? There were perfectly good fitting rooms just paces away. He knew plenty of inhibited women that could barely endure the community fitting room experience, but he couldn't imagine this girl being one of them.

By the time Blondie was trying on her second pair of shorts, Jack had adjusted his set of security perch moral protocols, discarding his integrity like he was a pigeon taking a crap.

Although the girl was no more than twelve feet away—if a crow

33

could fly through glass—he wanted to test the binoculars. She seemed flawless from where he sat; he had to know if she was as perfect up close.

After wiping the lenses clean with his shirt, and with a quick nudge to the focus wheel, he was inches from her skin. Starting at the base of her delicate neck, where her heavy blonde locks pranced like disobedient children, he panned down her arching back, slowly, absorbing every inch of her magnified, exaggerated, creamy skin.

He reached the bottom of her back, or the start of her bottom—he wasn't sure which label he preferred. The narrow channel was shallow there, widening and deepening as he probed further south. The binoculars were trained so hard to her skin that Jack had to brace them on his knees to keep the image steady. He was flirting with her most intimate spaces, her tempting nooks and crannies. A flaxen trail of fine down guided him through the crevice of her cheeks, and then further, to the bubble of gathered creases and folds between her legs.

Jack was enjoying the blonde and her unusual partiality toward public nudity—almost as much as she was enjoying it herself. As she bent and spread her body, and tugged and pulled at the shorts she wanted to try, he could see she was moist. The binoculars couldn't lie from this short distance. She was turning herself on as she moved from one pair of shorts to the next. What a beautiful, unusual vice for a woman to have, Jack thought.

But Blondie wasn't the only one becoming aroused. Jack had a pulsing hard-on that pressed for adjustment beneath the zipper of his khakis. He reached inside his boxers and pulled his swollen cock toward his belly, eliminating some of the pressure. But his prick was too full to be locked up in such a small prison, or, more appropriately, penal institution; the tip poked at the waist of his shorts like a dog begging for a walk. He considered unzipping his pants to let his cock out of the cage, but he knew he'd be tempted to wrestle with it, and that was one can of worms, or worm, he did not want to open. He opted instead to watch the blonde wrestle with her shorts.

It had become a silent movie of sorts—a silent porn movie. Jack couldn't hear the girl through the thick walls and mirrored glass, but he didn't need to. All he needed was for her to try on more shorts. She was happy to oblige.

The girl remained hunkered down as she changed outfits, rising only to scout fresh merchandise. She'd been pretty consistent with her method, selecting her pieces and returning to the same spot under Jack's window to try them on. But, with some new selections in hand, she decided to change things up a little. Instead of facing away from Jack toward the front of the store, she crouched and faced the back wall, providing him a fresh perspective, and a new level of excitement.

This time, Jack could see all the things up close that he hadn't before. He realized the binoculars were probably going to leave permanent rings around his eyes, but he kept them pressed against his face anyway. When Blondie slid out of her shorts, or rather J. Annie's shorts, he was there, zooming in on her luscious pussy, touring her tightly trimmed curls that rose in a thin puff of smoke above her cleft. She was definitely wet. Her lips were glistening and somewhat parted, and he could see inside her, all the way to her nectar-coated soul.

With her ass planted on the floor, the girl slipped into a different pair of shorts. She buttoned them, but she did not zip them. She remained on the floor with her legs thrust apart, and her knees bent. Jack was intrigued by this deviation in her otherwise predictable behavior. She didn't stand up to check the fit, or search for more clothes to try on. Instead, she slipped one hand through the open zipper, her fingers pressing on until they had vanished. The way her thin wrist jutted out from her shorts made it seem as if she had a giant erection.

Jack scrutinized the denim that had swallowed her hand. It quivered with a rhythmic fury, like a small mouse trying to escape a trap. Blondie wasn't adjusting herself. She was doing herself—while wearing a pair of J. Annie's finest.

Jack couldn't take it anymore. He wanted to fuck her. He wanted to suck her fingers dry, and then lick that beautiful pussy of hers. More than anything, he wanted to shove his hard dick deep inside her. He wanted to hear her moan in his ear—and he would wait for her to come. And when she did, when he could feel her tighten around him, he would liberate his shackled load. He would launch stream after pulsing stream of his hot milk deep into her gash, and she would cry out for more. And he would give it to her.

But that's not what he would do. He didn't have the guts, or he didn't have the confidence, or he wasn't that stupid, or maybe he just wanted to keep his job. What he *would* do was soak up as much of her performance as he could, be grateful for the imperishable memory, and then have Joel send the shorts she'd been playing with back to the warehouse as damaged merchandise.

Joel. The second Jack thought of him he spotted him, watching, partially obscured from the girl by a tall dress rack, and sporting a seriously flushed face. He had a floor level ticket to the show, and based on the way his hands were unsubtly crisscrossed over his crotch, a nirvana level plank in his pants.

Jack wasn't surprised that Joel had found the girl. He *was* surprised that nobody else had. He almost wished an unsuspecting customer had stumbled upon her as she finger fucked herself senseless. Maybe an orgy would have broken out. It wasn't like the day could get any more implausible.

Blondie still had her hand down her shorts, but she was done. Jack watched her chest rise and fall with a metered, purposeful pace. Although he couldn't see her fingers, he could tell where they were, what they were doing. He wished they were *his* fingers massaging her pussy gently, *his* fingers bringing her back to earth with a soft parachute landing.

"Jack Timmons to the office please, Jack Timmons to the office." The page sounded a little muffled, at least from the isolated security perch, but the message was loud and clear. Cherry needed him for something.

Jack glanced down at his still suffering dick. It hadn't retreated one bit. The tip winked at him like a one-eyed panhandler pleading for a chance. This was not the time to give in to its demands.

Jack took a deep breath and stood up in the perch to nudge his prick back in place—as best he could. His erection refused to go away without a fight. Somewhere in the uncontrollable recesses of his mind, his hamstrung snake was hoping it might still have a chance with the masturbating girl on the sales floor.

"Jack Timmons to the office please, Jack Timmons to the office."

The page seemed more insistent this time. Cherry's voice came through loud and clear. There must be an issue with a customer, Jack thought.

He had to leave the perch. Cherry knew where he was. She'd come and get him if he wasn't in the office soon.

Edging down the narrow metal staircase one clanking step at a time, all Jack could think about, all he could hope for, was that Blondie had left the store. How could he face her? It would be impossible, he decided. He shouldered the door open just a smidge, and peered toward where the girl was, or hopefully, had been.

He didn't see her sprawled across the tiles. He didn't see her shopping for another orgasm-inducing pair of shorts. Instead, she was staring at him from two, maybe three arm lengths away, smiling, as if she knew about him and his secret booth. Of course she knew, Jack thought; how could she not notice the certain profile, the impolite bulge, in his pants.

She was even prettier without the darkened glass between them. Her eyes were a crystal blue, her hair a symphony of blonde, streaked with multiple hues of the gentle color. And then there was her post-orgasmic glow that revealed itself not as a badge of shame, but as a stamp of pride.

Jack didn't know what to say, or what to do. He wanted to compliment her, but he couldn't decide how that would turn out. He smiled back. "Is there anything I can help you with?" The words came out weak, but they sounded appropriate, businesslike.

"Yes. I'd like to purchase these, please."

She held up four pairs of denim shorts, each of them, in Jack's opinion, worthy of a best supporting performer award. The one in front, the last pair she had tried, was still unzipped. He wanted to grab them, carry them to the register for her. He wanted to feel their warmth, their steaminess. For a moment, he considered that he might be going over the edge. He had to get it together.

"Follow me. I'm heading that way." Jack started toward the checkout counter adjacent to the office, desperate to fill his mind with anything other than the blonde girl that was tracing close behind.

Chapter Five

"I've been paging you for like five minutes. Could you not hear me?" Cherry spit the words at Jack the second he entered the store's overdone, understaffed, bookkeeping office.

"No, I couldn't hear you! That's why I'm here. What is it?"

"Geez, you don't have to bite my ear off. I just needed to ask you some…oh, I understand. Sorry I disturbed you." Cherry smiled, but not at Jack's face. She was looking at his crotch.

"What? What are you talking about? What was it you needed to ask me?" Jack and his hard-on had been busted, and all he could do was try and move the conversation forward.

Cherry inched closer to Jack, like she wanted to whisper something. "Wow. Impressive." She stretched the words up and down several octaves, breathing them into his ear.

Jack took a step back. "Why did you page me? What is it you need?"

"Could we go into your office? I'd rather talk in there."

Jack shook his head, and then shrugged. In the thirty seconds they took to trek to his office, his baton had retreated to its customary, harmless state. "Alright already. What is it?"

"So, you know how I've been thinking about taking a night class? Well, I found one at Scottsdale Community College."

"Hey, that's great, Cherry—nothing wrong with furthering your education. But why the hell did you have to page me? This couldn't wait?"

"Umm, anyway, I kind of need my nights off now—at least, most of them. I can work all the mornings you want me to!"

"Most of them? You know corporate wants me working openings. Unless I work open to close, I can only be here one night a week. You and Julie are my only key holders."

"I know, I know," Cherry said. "I already talked to Julie about it. She said she doesn't mind working a few extra nights. She just wanted me to run it by you."

"Alright," Jack said. "Anything else? I have stuff to do."

"What are you doing?" Cherry asked. "Maybe I can help."

"I think I can handle this myself, thanks." Jack thought about saying something to Cherry about her pushing the boundaries of their relationship. He was the store manager, and she was the store supervisor. Flirting with the boss, and making reference to his penis size, was not part of her job description.

But, he didn't want to say anything, or at least the wrong thing, to her. Jack was still trying to work out in his mind how he could have the girl, sexually, and get away with it, professionally. If she were going to express interest in him, he had to at least consider the possibilities. On the one hand, he wished they could stay where they were, relationship-wise. She was a good worker, and she was more than fun to be around—and ogle. On the other hand, if he could do more than undress her with his eyes, well, he had to figure out the safest way to do that.

In the meantime, he really needed to jerk off. This had not been an easy week for him; J. Annie's had become a more frustrating environment than a strip club. At least in a strip club it was okay to look, it was okay to fantasize, and, for just a few bucks extra...

Jack's balls had been mass-producing seed faster than Monsanto, and he didn't need his boys busting down the door the next time Cherry and her camel toe wanted to chat. It was time for a prison break.

"If I spent more time with you, I could learn more," Cherry pleaded. "Don't you want me to be the best I can be?"

"Of course. I'll let you know when I'm doing something important. Meanwhile, why don't you take a spin through the fitting rooms—make sure everything's okay." Jack didn't wait for a response. He left his supervisor alone in his office and lurched toward the men's room—a deserted oasis—a safe port in a sea full of women.

Jack thrust the door to the men's room open with one hand. His other hand was on his zipper. The brightly lit room's lone urinal was located just inside the entrance, maybe two steps away. He didn't want, or need, to waste any time. At this point, he figured he could squeeze one out in about a minute.

He dug with enthusiasm through the opening in his boxers and pried his poor, tortured member from its evil, cotton captor. He quickly conjured up Blondie, her fast working fingers, and that sweet, velvety snatch they'd been buried in. He reassessed his ETA to less than a minute.

What Jack had failed to notice, what he had been foolishly unmindful of, was that his store supervisor had been close on his heels since he had left the office. In fact, she had followed him into the men's room.

"I thought you said you'd let me know when you were doing something important, " Cherry said, grinning at her boss.

"What the hell? What are you doing?" Jack fumbled with his thick prick, gracelessly stuffing it back into his pants as quickly as he could.

Cherry stood arrow straight, hands on hips, arms arrayed so as to direct Jack's vision toward her vee; it seemed to him an uncalled for, calculated display of insensitivity. "I'm watching you, that's all. Come on, let me see."

"Cherry, you can't do this…whatever it is you're doing. Could you leave?" Jack's abused package was safely garaged and now zippered.

"So, I guess I'm going about this the wrong way, huh? I've been trying to be discreet."

"Discreet? Are you fucking kidding me? You followed me into the fucking men's room!"

"Is it? Is it a fucking men's room?"

"Seriously. You need to leave. I can't do this." Jack *did* want to do this—desperately—whatever *this* might be. But it was so wrong, in so many ways. What if it were all a joke? What if she had a bet with the other girls that she could touch his prick? He wouldn't put it past her; he didn't know her that well, that way, yet. He could easily imagine a photo of his junk pinned to the wall of the employee's restroom. If he was going to mess around with her, he needed to make sure everything was cool. This wasn't the time—or the place.

"I just want to have some fun." Cherry chirped the words more than she spoke them.

"You know what?" Jack paused, wanting to make sure that what he was about to say wouldn't harm anyone. "How about Joel? He seems like he'd be a fun guy."

"With you, Jack. I want to have fun with you."

40

She sounded sincere. A sticky blend of elation and panic gushed through Jack like a shot of hundred-dollar scotch.

"The kid really needs to get laid, Cherry. I know you girls talk. Isn't at least one of them interested?"

"No. He's too weird. And dorky. He's a dork."

"He's a nice guy. Someone needs to pop his cherry—sorry—deflower the poor dude. Don't girls like to take a guy's virginity? Anyway, speaking of weird, do you think we, or you, could leave the men's room now?"

"I could." Cherry leaned in to the mirror above the men's room sink, like she was looking for something. "My jaw muscles are so out of shape." With that, she started working her mouth open and closed, open and closed. She looked like an expensive fish in a cheap aquarium.

"Okay, Cherry. I'm leaving now." Jack reached for the door handle.

"Wait! Watch this!"

Jack slipped out of the room as efficiently as he could. He did not want, or need, to see whatever twisted, pervy thing she had planned.

***

I think you'll enjoy this more than peddling yoga mats. Jack had never forgotten those perceptive, unvarnished words delivered by Mike Allen, his twitchy district manager, on the day of his interview. He could have just said *you won't fucking believe how strange a girl can get until you see her in a store full of stylish, cheap clothes.* Not that those words would have been more impactful at the time—just more accurate, more intriguing. It didn't matter if the girl were a shopper, or an employee, Jack thought. Something happens to their heads in a disturbing, crippling way, when they walk through the doors; a raw surface becomes exposed that most men never have the opportunity to…see.

Jack had already confronted more rawness than he could handle in one day, yet he still had an hour left in the store. As soon as Julie returned from dinner, he would bolt.

He had sent Cherry home early because the girl had refused to leave his side all day. She had lightened up on her sham advances, or overt horniness, or whatever the hell it had been, but she remained a magnet, attached to him as if he had a metal plate in his pants. He thought it best to give her a couple hours off, hoping she'd spend the time wisely—perhaps buying batteries for her vibrator.

"We have kind of a situation, Jack. Care to help?" Carrie stood in the doorway of Jack's office, arms folded across her chest, eyes rolled to the ceiling.

"What's wrong, Carrie? What can I do?"

"Come with me."

Carrie led her wary boss across the sales floor, sidestepping t-stands, four-ways, rounders, and waterfall racks all crowded with the latest, hottest, discounted clothing for young ladies. She stopped at the doorway of fitting room number two and pointed her thumb in that direction, as if she were hitching a ride.

"She's in there," Carrie said, rolling her eyes one more time.

"What am I supposed to do? I can't go in there."

"I told this girl that J. Annie's policy is to not allow bathing suits to be tried on without underwear. She doesn't believe me. She's tried on, like, six suits already."

Jack listened to Carrie babble on, airing her frustrations. He thought the world of the girl, who was regularly one of his store's top sales producers. She was not only good with customers, she was also dependable, bouncy, and bright. Her only real fault, at least in Jack's opinion, was that she hadn't learned how to be subtle. He was sure her parents had never explained the difference between inside voice and outside voice to her. She was a loud girl—which wasn't always a bad thing—just sometimes. For instance, the customer she had been describing to Jack was now standing next to him, hands on hips, a scowl across her face, a tiny, pink, two-piece tight against her hot little body.

"Are you the manager?" the girl asked, maintaining her scowl.

"I'm Jack Timmons. Pleasure to meet you, miss…"

"Agitated. You can call me agitated."

"Well, I'm sorry to hear that. Maybe I can explain why we have a policy regarding trying on bathing suits without undergarments…" As Jack rattled through his oft-repeated bathing suit sermon, he took the opportunity to scan Ms. Agitated, and the one she was wearing.

The suit was cute. The girl was cuter. Jack pegged the fiery, pixie-tall brunette with plump tits, firm thighs and compact ass to be twentyish. He pegged his tormented sack of balls to be bluish.

"I don't really want to hear it. I know the law." As she spit out the words, the girl's face screwed into a rigid scowl, and her dark eyes shot machine gun daggers. It was as if she were arguing about something important.

"This isn't about the law, Ms…it's company policy. Now, I'd be happy to give you a…"

"Hey, listen to me." Ms. Agitated had heard enough. "In case you aren't aware, Mr. Manager, bathing suit bottoms come with removable protective strips—so that I don't have to try them on with underwear! See?"

Of course Jack would see. The cute little bitch really wanted him to. That's why she had bothered to pull the bikini bottom down to her knees. That's why she had bothered to point an angry finger toward the narrow strip of paper lining the crotch, which read, *Hygienic Protection For Fitting Purposes.* And that's why Jack was staring, open-mouthed, at a perfectly smooth, deliciously seductive pussy.

"Yes, I'm aware of the slits—I mean strips. But it's not, um, they're not, you know, our company policy doesn't allow for those, or, I mean, for you to only use those…"

"What Mr. Timmons is trying to saaay…" Carrie used a tempered version of her clearly audible voice as she attempted to save her boss. She could tell he was losing it—and she wasn't a rocket scientist. "…is that if you insist on trying a bathing suit on in our store, you must try it on over something. Otherwise, sorry we couldn't do business."

Until Carrie had opened her mouth, Jack had forgotten she was standing right next to him. He couldn't look at her now, because he knew she'd been looking at him. He was like an icicle, unable to move, dripping from the heat.

Ms. Agitated shimmied the bikini back up with an *hmmpf*, her legs shifting back and forth as the tiny pink bottoms headed north; Jack drank in every second of the journey.

"I'm leaving for the day, Carrie. Julie should be back from dinner, um, very soon. And…thank you. Thank you for your help." With his head down—because he wanted to avoid contact with

anyone—and his other head up—because he had surrendered control
of it to the store, Jack struck out for his office. If his car keys weren't
in his desk drawer, he would have just walked out the front door.
"Zhock! Zhock! Oh, goot! Am I too olt for zees blouse?"
Jack did not look up. He wanted to pretend that he did not hear
Evi screaming at him. He wanted to pretend that he could not see her
out of the corners of his eyes running toward him, her giant melons
bouncing like balls at an NBA game. He wanted to go home—take
care of things—get his head together. Evi would be back. And so
would Jack.

Chapter Six

J. Annie's always seemed so fresh and untainted in the morning, at least to Jack. Before the rows of glowing, recessed LED's, and shining, halogen track lights clicked on, and before the front doors were unlocked, he was able to breathe, his day not yet wilted from the crush of complications.

This was the calming, reassuring snapshot that flicked through Jack's mind as he parked his car deep in the lot, far from the store—where all good employees parked.

As he approached the store, keys in hand, Jack scanned for Emily and Trish, the morning prep crew, but they weren't milling about by the door as usual. He had never known them to be late to work. In fact, they were always early—unlike Cherry, the girl who must have let them in.

"Hi Jack!" Cherry greeted him as he entered the store, wearing both of her usual, vivid smiles.

"Hi Cherry. I wasn't expecting you for another half hour or so. What's the occasion?"

"I wanted to get some things done. And I wanted to be sure I had a chance to apologize for my behavior yesterday. I guess I was just in a…mood."

"Thanks, Cherry. I appreciate it."

What Jack had almost said was, "I appreciate you", but he quickly fixed his words to something a little less personal, a little more generic. He still wanted her, but he hadn't quite thought of a way to have her—discreetly. Actually, he'd spent most of the previous evening thinking of ways to have her—while he was having her—single-handedly.

"So, what do we have going today?" Cherry seemed full of energy, ready to take on the world, or at least the daily schedule.

"Well, we're supposed to be receiving a big shipment from the warehouse today. Eight cartons. Could you make sure Joel stays on top of that?"

"Yeah, I'll make sure he stays on top—of the shipment."

"C'mon, Cherry. We're starting fresh today, right? Why don't you work on the schedule? I've got some paperwork to deal with. Now scoot, get out of here—please?"

"Aw, I love it when you say please. I'll go take care of it—sir."

Jack had an underlying motive for assigning his supervisor a task, and kicking her out of his office: he had to pee.

Although Cherry had apologized for her anomalous, forward behavior of the previous day, he'd been around this block before, and he definitely didn't want her watching him take a whiz. She'd already started in on the double-entendres, and the store wasn't even open yet.

Jack scurried to the men's room, flipped on the lights, and reached into his pants.

"Hey, big boy!"

"What the hell, Cherry! I can't even pee by myself?"

"You don't have to! Let me help." Cherry lunged for Jack's open zipper and began to wrestle him for access.

It was the most bizarre act of carnal insolence that Jack had ever experienced—and he'd spent years with his ex, Rebecca—a certified nut.

A hot, aggressive girl was doing everything in her power to grab his dick and wrench it from his pants. When she pinched his ass with the pointy nails of her other hand, he flinched—and she won.

It didn't matter now to Jack. His twenty-year-old supervisor had her hand wrapped around his prick. If that's what she needed to do to win her little bet, fine. If she just wanted to see it for her own fucked-up reasons, fine. Either way, it was over. Cherry got what she wanted.

But, Cherry wasn't done. He thought he detected some drool at the edge of her lips when she began talking again. "Go ahead, pee. I'll hold it for you."

"No, no, no...no. I don't even have to go any more. I'm so sorry."

"Alright, then." With one hand still wrapped around his warm cock, she began to massage it, and stroke it. "You need to pull these down." Her other hand tugged at the waist of his pants.

"Excuse me?"

"So, you still think nothing's happening here? C'mon—off with these."

Jack was not ready to cooperate—not yet. His penis, however, was on a different page; through Cherry's adroit ministrations, it thickened quickly—from anxiously lifeless—to timber grade. It didn't help Jack's case that Cherry's hovering, full tits were inches away, taunting him unsympathetically as they strained against her stretchy, red top. Her nipples kept pace with his own hardness, and he wanted so desperately to rub his thumbs over them, expose them, and suck them into his mouth—a gift to his yearning, surging tongue.

Cherry yanked Jack's pants down to his knees. He followed her as she bent, waves of auburn hair, and giant, penned-in tits filling his eyes.

She slid her grip down to the base of his cock, and then tiptoed her lips over the balance of his shaft. She cupped his balls so she could feel their weight, their silkiness, their resilience. She began working it—all of it. Her mouth slurped and sucked at everything within its reach; her soft hand jerked at the parts that weren't. He was in her mouth, and he was in her hands.

Jack wanted to grab her so he could play with her, too. His hands had access to the top of her head, but that was all. He rolled his fingers through her thick, soft hair; the dense locks were heavy in his hands, and bobbed rhythmically with each energetic stroke.

Cherry was good. She was very good. Jack could tell she was into it, and that she hadn't been plotting some sort of hoax, or piece of mischief. She did want him—just like he wanted her.

Since Jack could see little of the girl as she went down on him, he closed his eyes and imagined her as if she were snared beneath his weight, her sprayed-on pants gone, her stretchy top melted away. She was firm all over—her heavy breasts, muscled thighs, glassy, unruffled abs, and cute, shapely ass—all steady and strong. What he didn't have to imagine was her warm, velvety mouth, snug around his prick.

Cherry wasn't about to stop, or give in. Not until Jack had given her what she had been so hungry for. He was close to delivering; his whole body stiffened, his eyes clamped shut as if vexed by a hurricane wind, and his skin bloomed to a bright rosy hue. She ratcheted up her already impassioned dance, pumping hard with her

47

fist and tonguing his swollen head with a savage lack of restraint. There was no returning now. The dam had ruptured, and the flood was imminent. With one more stroke of her hand and pass of her tongue, Cherry's persevering mouth filled full of his cream. One sticky surge after another rushed past her plump lips and sent her over the moon. If she were truly hungry for him, he was not going to disappoint. She milked his shaft, and drank him in until there was no more for him to give—at least for now.

Cherry tilted her head up, and Jack lowered himself to grab her shoulders and lift her to her feet. They stood apart, looking into each other's eyes. Jack wasn't sure what to say, or what to do.

"This is between us, Jack. Now, if you'll excuse me, I've got a store to open."

Jack wanted to say something but he struggled for the right words. Somehow *thank you* didn't seem appropriate. A kiss? Not now.

Cherry's hand was on the door when she turned and smiled at her boss. Jack drank her in one more time.

"By the way, thanks for letting me work morning shifts." Cherry winked, whirled, and then pranced out onto the sales floor.

***

It took Jack ten minutes to collect his thoughts and get himself together enough to leave the men's room. It wasn't that Cherry's assault came out of left field or anything, but it did take him by surprise—a literal grab him by the balls eye-opener.

But now the bridge had been crossed, the ice shattered, and the bottle uncorked. There was no undoing what had been done. The question was, would there be any doing of what had yet to be done?

By the time Jack left the men's room, Cherry had the store unlocked, the lights on, and the machine that was J. Annie's open and running.

Jack edged onto the brightly lit sales floor and began colorizing a rack of Capri pants, like he'd been busy tidying up the place all morning. He had no reason to fear extra scrutiny, or sideways glances from his staff. He would have normally been concealed inside his office anyway this time of day, insulated from the preopening hubbub. But, it made him feel better to be doing something, even if it was just a little something. It wasn't as if he was splashing about in a puddle of guilt. So what if he'd spent the last half hour getting blown by the store supervisor? Nobody got hurt, and nobody had to know.

Despite being confident that his little dalliance had gone unnoticed, Jack scanned the room, just to make sure no one was pointing, gesturing, or giggling his way. The store was still pretty quiet, with just a few early customers milling about. One of them seemed to be darting quickly from one rack to another, like a hummingbird scouting for nectar.

The quirky-cute young flutterer with shiny black hair landed at a display table one row from Jack's, and began thumbing through a stack of jeans. Jack snagged a great view of her tramp stamp—a small, rose-colored heart, the tip of which pointed suggestively toward the cleft of her ass. The somewhat misty image hovered lure-like above a pair of tight, faded, low-rise jeans.

Usually, when Jack was sexually drained, he would give his eyes a break before reverting to his standard, lustful deportment. But, there was something intriguing about this slender girl that made him want to…see more.

As she filtered through the jeans, Jack was treated to the full landscape. A slight girl, her huge boobs, though extraordinary, seemed out of place—unnatural, Jack decided. Her body was shaped like a slice of pie, crust side up. If not for the negligible interruption of her modest hips, she had the profile of a perfect vee.

The girl had an adorable face, Jack surmised, despite her possible overindulgence at the makeup counter. Her long, straight hair was gathered in the back with a large, red clip that appeared mouth-like, its big pointy teeth grabbing at her head like some sort of perverted monster. It wasn't an accessory Jack had seen before—nor was she a girl Jack had seen before.

Jack decided he would do the right thing and approach her to see if she were in need of any assistance. He eased toward her, allowing time to savor her unique, buxom visage. As he approached, he noticed her sliding a folded pair of pricey jeans into her generously proportioned shoulder bag. A second pair quickly followed.

This was not what Jack wanted to see, or wanted to deal with.

But, as much as he hated doing it, he knew that capturing the bad guys was part of the gig. His mind rushed to concoct a plan of action.

"Excuse me, Miss, is there anything I can help you with?" Jack tried to maintain eye contact as he spoke, but her boobs were even more surreal up close; even blinders would have been worthless.

"I am just fine, thank you! Actually, I am looking for this pair in a size six. I wonder if you would be a doll and check the stock room for me?"

The girl waved a random pair of jeans at the store manager while spilling her words with a somewhat affected, likely fake, Southern drawl. Jack would have been impressed, if she weren't a fucking thief.

"Sorry, we don't have any back stock. But, are you sure you're a six? I saw you put a couple size fours in your bag. Would you like me to hold those for you while you shop?"

"Well, I just don't know *what* you are talking about. I'll be fine. I'm just waiting for my friend. She should be along any time now, so I think I'm just going to browse for a bit. Thank you, you're so sweet!"

The shoplifter behaved as if the last five minutes of her life had been magically erased, and that there wasn't a cloud in the sky. She started shopping her way toward the front of the store, pawing through the occasional rack of clothes, pretending not to notice that Jack was close on her heels.

Jack couldn't take his eyes off the girl, or, more specifically, her shoulder bag—not even for a second. But he needed a partner—someone that could witness whatever was about to go down. He couldn't break his gaze. If he did, he wouldn't be able to bust her. What if she ditched the pilfered jeans while he wasn't looking? When he searched her bag, he'd be nothing but screwed.

The only store employee in Jack's line of sight was Joel, who was busy restocking a rack of skirts. Jack thought he'd be an excellent choice; the young man's eyes would never leave this woman. He'd be looking at her tits, but that would be close enough. Jack grabbed a piece of Joel's shirt and nodded toward Ms. Purloin. Joel fell in step behind his boss.

They had reached the front of the store when the girl stopped in her tracks. Jack waited for her decision. If she dumped the items and ran, fine. She'd most likely never return. If she were stupid enough to go for it, Jack would have to do his thing.

Apparently, her giant boobs weren't filled with brains. The girl didn't take a deep breath; she didn't screw-up her face in a display of strained courage. She simply walked to the door and reached for the handle.

"I don't think so," Jack said, his voice plain and clear. "Come with me."

Jack led the girl by her elbow to his office. Joel shadowed their steps, his gaze fixed to the small, rose-colored heart etched above her splendid ass.

"Have a seat, Miss…" Jack held the "sss" as long as he could, but she was holding out.

"I don't have to tell you," the girl growled.

"Oh, I think you do." Jack spilled the contents of the girl's shoulder bag across his desk. "You see, I have a report that I have to fill out, and there's a space just waiting for your name. It'll make things a lot easier when the cops get here, too. Trust me, none of us wants to do any paperwork. Let's just be cooperative, huh?"

"Tiffany—my name's Tiffany. And you don't need to call the po-po—okay?"

"Yes, I do. Give me just a second here, Tiffany. Don't move."

Jack motioned Joel to the far side of his office, then whispered to him: "We need to be beyond reproach here, Joel. Listen—stay in here with me. Don't leave. Don't speak. If I'm left alone with her, she may say I tried to touch her inappropriately, or something.

"She smells like bubblegum, Jack."

"I know, I know. Listen; just stand here and watch." Jack grabbed Joel's shoulders and pushed down a little, like he was planting him. Then he planted himself at his desk, across from Tiffany.

"First time here, Tiffany?" Jack used his grim, stern voice. He noticed it could use a little dusting.

"My first time—and my last. I promise. I swear to you."

Jack glared at her, trying to decide if she had any hostility, or drugs, in her.

"Listen. Maybe we can work something out," Tiffany said, arching her thin eyebrows high, and leaving them there. "You know who I am. Maybe we can do a little bartering."

"I'm sorry, Tiffany. Have I seen you before?"

"Really? I was sure you were a fan, the way you were leering at me. I was actually kind of flattered. I haven't worked in a few years, and I'm not recognized so much any more. You know, *Breakfast In Tiffany, Craving Tiffany, Tiffany's Treasures, Behind Tiffany All The Way*...I could go on—and on."

"You're a, um, I'm not sure the proper..."

"Porn star. Yeah, that's me. Well, it was me. So, listen, Mr. J. Annie's, how about I get naked for you, maybe wash away some of that toughness you're wearing like last night's top sirloin."

Tiffany didn't wait for an answer. One of her hands stretched to remove her red plastic hair clip, while the other unbuttoned her overtaxed crop top. Like a good pro, her hair was down and her top was off in seconds. Her chest popped out like it was spring loaded.

"Listen, Tiffany," Jack couldn't help but stare at the prodigious hydrants pointed his way as he spoke. "No. Don't do this. And your timing is horrible, by the way."

Whatever Jack was muttering did not seem to matter to Tiffany. She shimmied out of her tight jeans like a snake shedding its skin. She was as naked as the day she shot *Tiffany's Fine Asp*, and, from what Jack could see, she hadn't lost any of her venom.

"Come on, baby," the porn luminary said, employing her most sultry, beseeching voice, "Let's do it."

Tiffany wasn't about to stand there, motionless, like a thick filet of sushi grade ahi waiting to be admired. She began writhing, and bending, and when she was doubled over—her head at her ankles—she spread her ass cheeks wide, giving Jack a doorstep view of her immaculate, flawless playground.

"I love anal, you know—or maybe you don't. I can never seem to get enough." Her ass and her head turned Jack's way. Her eyelids were clamping together, as if she were contemplating her orgasm.

Jack swallowed hard. He was sure if the crap from her purse weren't spread out all over his desk that she'd be dancing on it by now. This was wrong. Everything about it was wrong. It was too late at this point, but he should have had Cherry in here with him, or at least one of the other girls. His keeping beyond reproach idea was history—tossed in the garbage and set aflame the second Joel had closed the office doors.

Joel—Jack had almost forgotten the poor guy was in the room. The young man had been stone still and silent, just as his boss had requested. Jack glanced over at him. He seemed paralyzed, his posture rigid straight—like a toy soldier. Jack didn't have to look close to notice the big party under way in Joel's pants; the tent was quite large. Jack did not want to think about, or see, the guest list.

Jack was fucked. He knew it. He was fucked by the naked girl in his office with the big tits, hot ass, and slick, bald pussy. His options were limited.

"Listen," Tiffany moaned, "you can tell all your friends how you fucked a porn star. Give it to me. Come on. Give it to me."

"No, you listen to me," Jack sputtered out the words weaker than he had intended. "You will never set foot in this store again, got it?"

"Promise. Now, how do you want it? Back door? Hmm?"

"I don't want it at all," Jack said, his balls tapped out, but his conscience somehow functioning. "How about him?" Jack nodded toward his petrified stock supervisor, who looked ready to hurl, pass out, or blow a wad in his pants at the slightest breeze.

"Um, no, I don't think so. You, yes—him, I might kill him. I think he needs medical attention, don't you?"

"Okay…now look, this is your warning. If I see you in my store again, I'm calling the cops. Got it?"

Tiffany threw her clothes on almost as quickly as she'd removed them. "Got it. And, hey, thanks. Oh, and Google me sometime, okay? You might appreciate me more when you're…alone."

Jack escorted the erotic film actress to the door, leaving Joel some time to recover, and shake a few things from his head.

Chapter Seven

Jack thought he was being clever, asking Julie to switch schedules with him for the day. He'd work the closing shift, and Cherry and Julie would open. He'd still get to spend time with Cherry, but during the busy afternoon—the less likely to be assaulted part of the day.

What he hadn't counted on, what he had forgotten about, was that he had promised Cherry some extra hours this week. And, of course, this was the day she'd chosen to work from open to close. Jack was reminded of this the minute he slinked as furtively as he could into his office to catch up on some paperwork.

"Hey, Jack!" Cherry shouted, causing her boss to flinch, "I almost didn't see you come in. So, don't worry, you didn't miss much this morning. We got a big shipment from the warehouse, but Joel's been knocking it out. I've never seen the boy with so much energy. Anyway, don't forget I'll be working with you tonight! It'll be fun!"

Jack's eyes rolled and his prick twitched at the same time. "Sounds great, Cherry. I'm going to need Joel to help me with a small floor move, but I promise not to keep him long. Could you ask him to meet me in fitting room four? I need to get some racks out of there, and I could use his help."

"No prob, boss! He should almost be done with the shipment anyway. Anything else?"

Cherry flashed her bright smile and placed her hands on her hips, as if coaxing Jack to select from her daily menu of appetizing bits and pieces. He scanned the bill of fare, and, despite craving the mouth-watering slice of pie that sat front-and-center on her dessert tray, informed her that he didn't need anything else at the moment.

Jack grabbed the corporate-dictated plan-o-grams, or, as he thought of them, maps for idiots who couldn't even arrange their own sock drawer, and made his way to fitting room four.

For as long as Jack had been with J. Annie's, fitting room four had been used as kind of a catch all space. Since each of the community fitting rooms could easily accommodate twenty shoppers at a time, there had never been a need for this room, at least not as it was originally purposed. Jack often wondered what sort of optimism the architect had been snorting when he designed the place. The number of shoppers in the store might occasionally exceed sixty, but a fitting room to a woman was kind of like a lady's powder room to a man—best not to enter, unless absolutely necessary. Dressing room four was good for at least something, unlike, say, the male nipple: it was the perfect place to stash shit, like surplus store fixtures.

After rolling aside the formidable, chrome-plated, *Sorry, Room Closed* sign, and unhooking the thick stanchion rope that served as sentry and seemed more suited to a trendy nightclub's entryway, Jack pulled open the final barrier, the curtains. He stepped into the room and immediately stubbed his foot on a t-stand rack that had toppled over—months earlier.

"Shit!" Jack tried to mute his scream as he scrambled to stay upright. "Holy cra…what's going on in here?"

About eight feet and three empty, shiny, chrome racks away from Jack, two naked, athletically toned young women were wrapped in a curious embrace. One of them was lying face-up on a low, wooden bench, her legs straddling the narrow piece. She seemed to be striving for purchase with both feet planted firmly on the floor. The other girl was on top, pointed the other direction, her flesh pressing against the girl beneath, her head buried between her thighs.

Jack's appearance did little to rattle the girls. They continued feasting on one another with a determined, undaunted resolve; the presence of a strange man was inconsequential to their goal. Jack wanted to speak up again, maybe a little louder, or stronger this time, but he thought they were close to coming, and he was hesitant to interrupt such a thing.

A pool of soft moans and dewy slurping sounds oozed through the room, but remained constant, unvarying. Jack watched and listened. Now it seemed to him that the girls could go on forever like this. He was okay with that. He rationalized in his mind that they were the trespassers, the violators, the intruders. He could stand here all day and breathe in this theater of Sapphic delights if he wanted.

The girl on top lifted slightly, perhaps for a gulp of air, or perhaps to shift her breasts, which had been huddled fast beneath her.

Jack spied her jiggling set of small, firm bullets for the first time, and his prick, which up till this moment had only filled to a modest, respectful proportion, hardened to capacity. He wanted desperately to lick the firm, taut buds that jutted from the girl's perfect little mouthfuls.

Jack imagined the parts hidden from his view, and he wanted to lick those too. He wanted to jump on top of the pile and reach in with his hands and his mouth and his aching cock. He wanted to feel everything they were feeling, and taste everything they tasted.

"Jack? You in there?" Joel whispered from outside the room, his cheek flush against the curtain.

"Yeah buddy, hang on." Jack whispered back, reluctant now to disrupt the two girls. He looked around for some object, or some detail to distract him, and deflate him. Instead, he saw their reflection in the mirrors that ringed the room. They appeared as one billowing, swelling ripple of female flesh—and then suddenly they stopped. They both turned their heads toward Jack. The one on the bottom spoke.

"We don't mind if you watch. It's okay."

Jack grabbed at the curtain behind him, and pulled it aside. He couldn't stay in the room. It was wrong, for so many reasons. He hated to waste the opportunity though. Someone with less at stake deserved to see this—someone that may have only seen this sort of thing on a small computer screen in a likely dim room with an even more likely box of tissues nearby. Jack lifted a finger to his lips.

"Go take a look, Joel. There's something going on in there you don't see everyday. Don't upset them. Just watch."

Joel nodded as he inched in to the room, tentatively. Jack kept an eye on the young man, making sure he didn't start screaming, or pass out.

Joel crept forward, his arms spread, his body slightly hunched over. He looked like he was trying to corner a wounded animal. Jack couldn't watch anymore. He pulled the curtains closed and stood guard over the entryway, hoping he hadn't just ruined a perfectly good employee.

"What's going on, Jack? Did Joel not show up to help you yet? I told him like fifteen minutes ago that you…"

"Shhh, Cherry, he's in the room. You would absolutely not

believe what the hell is going on in there."

"I want to see, I want to see. C'mon, Jack, let me in."

"I'm not so sure that's a great idea, Cherry. On the other hand, I'm thinking this sort of thing probably wouldn't faze you at all. Go ahead—stick your head in. But don't say a word."

Jack was certain that Cherry wouldn't find offense at, or be repelled by, two girls enjoying a little box lunch. He was almost as certain, that, at some point in her life, she'd dipped her tongue in a few honey jars herself. He waited patiently for her reaction.

"Oh my god, Jack! How did you do that? Where did you find those girls? How much did you pay them?"

"Ha! Very funny, Cherry. I walked into the room to find the racks I needed, and there they were! I was going to throw them out of the store, but they seemed very nice. They even said it was okay if I watched. How could I not let them have their fun?"

"Well, you are a saint, Jack Timmons. So, I don't know how you did it, but you did it good. And, holy shit, he's got maybe the largest penis I have ever seen. The thing is a weapon. Hey, it's a fucking weapon!"

Jack went pale as he tried to digest what Cherry was telling him. He thought Joel would enjoy watching a couple girls have at each other. He didn't intend for the young man to jerk off in the middle of fitting room four. Cherry had seen something she shouldn't have, and now Jack would have to contrive some sort of managerial response. He was sure the whole store would know within minutes that their stock supervisor was juicing his goose in one of the fitting rooms. He had to get Cherry to keep this to herself.

"Cherry, you didn't see anything, okay? I don't want this getting around. Promise me."

"I thought you'd be proud, Jack. But, whatever. I'm pretty sure those two girls will be telling all their friends about it. I mean, that's almost a once in a lifetime thing."

"I have a feeling those girls have watched a guy jerk off before, Cherry. They seem…worldly?"

"Um, they're not exactly watching Joel beat his meat, Jack. Maybe you wanna take a look."

Cherry stared at her boss, radiating enough smugness to power a small village. Jack was hesitant to peek through the curtain, afraid that whatever perverted thing he might witness would get lodged in his memory and never evaporate.

As much as he hated to do it, he knew he had to look. Jack pealed back a corner of the curtain, prepared to recoil at the slightest glimpse of Joel's anatomy, and poked his head in. He blinked hard several times, trying to make sure he was getting the correct image from his apparently fucked up eyes.

Joel was banging one of the girls. Or, more precisely, she was banging him. Spread naked on the same narrow bench the girls had been keeping sloppy-warm, Joel looked like some sort of sex slave. He was on his back, legs splayed, and feet firm to the floor. The trim girl with the small, straightforward tits was riding him, her feet also on the floor, her ass aimed at his face. She leaned back somewhat as she bobbed up and down on his prick, or at least part of his prick. She didn't seem able, or willing, to take in all of him.

The other girl had straddled Joel's greedy mouth and was rolling her hips back and forth over his insatiable tongue. The tips of her fingers slapped gently, rapidly against her clit, and her face at once displayed an unexpected, crazed veneer. The three of them spun like a well-oiled machine of pistons, rods, pumps, and valves. The girl's soft moans had given way to shrill cries, and Jack, for the first time, was grateful for the store's piped-in, up-tempo music. Somehow the volume kept a decibel or two above their growing whimpers.

"My turn," the girl on Joel's face announced with a sudden jolt of assertiveness.

Jack wished he had spun from them then and pulled his head back to the real world side of the curtain. He wished he had left the girls the way they were, the way they were supposed to be, the way he wanted to remember them. He wished he had never let Joel into the room.

The girl with the exquisitely uncomplicated tits lifted herself from Joel's cock, her ass wriggling up his chest until all of him had been released. Jack recalled a scene from a campy horror film that was uncomfortably similar to the scene that was rolling now. But this wasn't some monster-sized constrictor swallowing a young, nubile, oblivious girl. This was a nubile, young girl that had swallowed an oblivious, monster-sized constrictor. Unfortunately, or fortunately, depending on perspective, Joel's massive penis was not the work of some Hollywood special effects master.

Jack couldn't help but stare at the foot long beast as the girls switched places. He had never given it much thought, but if forced to guess he would have said that whatever Joel was packing had been rubbed away from years of abuse. Unless Joel's dick had previously been a tree, this was just another of Jack's wide of the mark presumptions. He wondered how the guy kept the thing hidden all this time.

The second girl eagerly mounted Joel, somehow accommodating all of him. Her full breasts bounced at a measured pace as she sprang high then plummeted down onto the colossus. Her juices trickled over her firm thighs, and her skin flushed with spatters of crimson. Her cries pitched higher and more insistent as she contemplated her orgasm. Jack could see how much she was savoring every inch of his stock supervisor. He guessed she enjoyed riding horses.

Jack couldn't believe that Joel hadn't shot his wad yet, though he considered he may already have gotten off, discreetly, once or twice inside the first babe; after all, he was a young, horny guy who finally got his paws on a couple of young, horny girls. Regardless, Jack did not want to be around for the fireworks. He stepped away from the curtain with a sense of pride over Joel and his achievement, and with a sense of astonishment over how fucking amazing a stupid clothing store could be.

Jack fully expected Cherry to be waiting for him, arms folded, a told you so grin fixed to her face. She was nowhere in sight, though, which did not bother Jack one bit. This was a business, after all, and there was always something, or someone, that needed tending to.

Chapter Eight

"I just want to remind you, Jack, that it's five o'clock. I'm leaving at six. If you're going to get anything for dinner, you might want to take care of that."

"What? Oh, thanks, Julie. I'm a little behind with my paperwork so I'm just going to hang out here in my office, maybe grab a bag of pretzels out of the machine. Thanks for the heads up, though. Listen—while you're here, I want to make sure you're okay about working more nights. Cherry told me you're good with it, but I don't want you to..."

"I'm good, Jack. Don't worry. She'd do the same for me, I'm sure."

"Well, you're a sweet girl, Julie. Why don't you knock off now, get out of here early for a change. I'm not going anywhere, and Cherry should be back from dinner in a few minutes anyway. Go on. I'm giving you a one hour paid vacation from this place."

"Um, sure, I guess. I'll just wait for Cherry, and then I'll take off."

"No need to wait. Get out of here while you've got the chance. Now scoot!"

Julie seemed hesitant to leave, but she had always been that sort of worker—dedicated, devoted, by the book. As she shuffled reluctantly from his office, Jack couldn't help but glare at her cute butt. She still was, and probably always would be, one of his fantasy babes. He loved her girl-next-door persona: the sweet disposition bordering on angelic, the loyalty to a fault—the shatterproof morals. But scarcely concealed beneath all of that goodness and purity were pieces of Julie that he couldn't ignore, that he wanted to run his hands over, or through.

But, Jack knew better than to go there. Julie was the ideal assistant manager, and he didn't want to ruin their easy and practical alliance. Plus, he wasn't exactly looking for a new filling station. Although Cherry wasn't offering full service yet, she was quite good at the pump. Jack was more than satisfied.

The store's break room was across the sales floor from Jack's office. On his way to and from his pretzel run, he stopped to chat-up several of his employees. All of them were busy twiddling their thumbs—nothing more. He could smell a slow and tedious evening ahead.

Jack settled in behind his desk, popped open a Coke, and ripped into his bag of Tiny Twists. He hadn't been back in his office for more than a minute, when he heard a sharp tapping on his door.

"Hey, Jack!" Cherry squealed, as if she hadn't seen him in years. "Mind if I bother you?"

"Sure—bother me all you want, Cherry."

"Ooh, I like that attitude. Is that supposed to be your dinner? A bag of pretzels?"

"Yeah. I didn't really feel like going anywhere, and I've got to finish filling out some capital expenditure request crap, so, here I am. You have a good dinner?"

"I did, thanks. I *am* still a little hungry though. I'm thinking of having a little dessert?"

"Are you asking me?"

Cherry locked the office door, then strolled, tart-like, around Jack's desk till she was in his face—or rather till her remarkably detailed camel toe was in his face.

"Wait. What the hell are you thinking, Cherry?"

"I'm thinking you're going to get your pants off, so I can get you off. Don't make me beg."

"I can't, we can't do this. Not here, not now."

"I locked the door, Jack. Besides, I'm pretty sure you won't last long, not after that little show you watched earlier. Pretty hot, huh? Two good looking babes getting it on with Godzilla."

"Actually, it was just two girls, at least for a while, before I let, um…"

"Either way, Jack, are you going to unbuckle, or am I going to have to do it for you?"

Jack's face was inches from Cherry's easily understandable, unambiguously cloaked crotch. A burst of fragrance—something spicy and incredibly sensual—something she likely purchased at the "seduce your boss" store, hit him at once.

"What are we going to do?" Jack asked, leering at her masked pussy.

M.L. Joslyn

"I," Cherry clung to the word like she wasn't sure what to say next, "am going to suck you hard…and then we'll see…we'll see what happens."

Jack looked around his office, nervously, as if someone else could have snuck in without him noticing. His gaze returned to the soft-core marvel of Cherry's paper-thin pants, the arc of her firm, forceful thighs, and the unmistakable lines of her female composition. He unzipped his pants and slid them to the floor.

Cherry reached inside Jack's boxers, her hands exploring everywhere, touching everything. She pulled his shorts down till they nested inside his pants then pitched them, along with his loafers, under his desk.

Cherry was on her knees, her legs spread for balance, her plump lips grazing the tip of Jack's thick cock. She took him into her mouth and then allowed her tongue to explore up and down his shaft, over and around his small slit. She cradled his sack with soft fingers, while her auburn tresses frolicked in his lap.

When Jack was fully erect, Cherry sat back to admire her achievement. She seemed spellbound by his full rod, measuring the cadence of its subtle pulsing with her focused eyes. With one hand caressing his balls, and the other stroking the soft hairs of his thigh, she looked to be deciding what to do next with her prize.

Without breaking her gaze, Cherry got to her feet and then pulled her knit blouse up and off. She rolled her head to and fro, evoking those girls in shampoo commercials who proudly flaunt their perfectly luxuriant, slow motion manes.

Jack was just a slinky white bra away from setting his eyes on Cherry's unreasonably large, perfectly poised breasts. It was tough for him not to stare. He had yet to see them as nature intended, stripped of all wrapping, uncontaminated by absurd fabrics. He at first thought it was somewhat inappropriate of him to be ogling her chest while waiting for the big unveiling. But, her eyes were still glued to his engorged prick, which, in his mind, was just as inappropriate. If there were ever a better example of tit-for-tat, he couldn't think of it.

Cherry reached to unhook her bra, her arms seemingly tethered behind her as if she were being cuffed. She appeared to be fumbling with the catch, unable to work it. Jack didn't understand what was taking her so long. In his experience, if a girl wanted her bra off, it was off. No girl had ever asked for his assistance—not that Cherry was asking now.

Jack was contemplating Cherry's almost unveiled tits, wondering how many more seconds it would take before he'd get to see them, touch them, and taste them. Suddenly, an unexpected jangling noise shattered the silent drama that had been mounting in the room. Someone was at his office door, wanting in.

"Oh, shit, thank you for locking the door," Jack whispered.

Cherry did not respond to Jack's skittish expression of gratitude, but she did stop toying with her bra. She remained composed and focused, putting her fingers to use on Jack's softening erection.

The noise came back, but this time it wasn't the rattle of a loose doorknob. It was the sound of a key, finding its way into a tumbler.

Jack's mind raced and his heart pounded. It was too late to do anything about his condition, his state of undress. He was fucked, but who was it that would be doing the fucking? Who was it that would be bringing his agreeable, unrealistic job to a screeching, messy termination? Nobody else had a key to his office.

But there *was* someone with a key—someone that might need access to files, or someone that might need a place to steal away for a few minutes. The pressures of running a store can sometimes get to a person.

"Good job, Cherry!" Julie used her pat-on-the-back voice, but ratcheted up the fieriness.

"Thanks, Julie. It wasn't easy."

"Do you think I should call Mr. Allen?"

"I don't know, Julie. What do you think, Jack?"

Jack couldn't answer. His assistant manager and his supervisor had conspired against him. Why would he ever want to talk to them again? He thought they'd been getting along great. He thought he had treated them well. He thought they had treated him well. Cherry was still treating him well. Her small fingers were, even now, wrapped around his prick, stroking it, pleading with it.

"I think it's time, Cherry. If we're going to fuck him, let's fuck him good."

Jack had never heard Julie use a profanity. He was more jarred by her use of the word "fuck," than by her sudden desire to take him down. He looked for her camera, or phone, or whatever she might be carrying that would photograph his withering erection, his demise.

"I don't think he gets it, Julie," Cherry said, her hands still beating a dead horse.

"I'm pretty sure I've never seen him this pale, Cherry. Jack, listen to me. I don't want to screw you...over. I want to fuck you. We both want to fuck you. Now."

Jack was speechless, which was probably a good thing for everyone. Julie walked around the desk, leaned in, and gave him a soft kiss on his lips. Her tongue pressed into his mouth, and then she quickly removed it, leaving Jack a swallow of mint and a swelling cock.

Julie kneeled next to Cherry and began stroking her thick hair with enthusiastic, yearning fingers. She guided Cherry's head to hers, and they pressed their lips together, gently at first, and then with the eagerness of two young lovers indulging their immodest hunger for one another. Jack listened to the dim murmur of their passion, and he could tell they'd been around this block more than once. He wondered what else he didn't know, what else he'd been missing.

"So, I think he's ready, Julie. What do you think?"

"It looks to me like his cock could use some attention. By the way, you were right Cherry—his is very nice, very...inviting. Do you want to hear what we're going to do to you, Jack? Or, do you want us to just...surprise you."

"I, uh, you girls do realize the store's open, right? What if..."

"Don't worry about any what if's," Julie interrupted. "I told Carrie we'd be in an urgent, closed door meeting, and not to disturb us. Enjoy this—okay?"

"Sure. Yeah. I will try my best to enjoy this. I promise. Wait - do I get a safe word?"

"You're a funny guy, Jack Timmons," Cherry said. "Relax, okay?"

The girls pulled each other off the floor, and then Julie leaned in toward her boss, close enough to graze his face with her own.

"We're going to get undressed now, if that's okay with you," Julie whispered, her breath brushing his cheek.

The girls huddled, slowly grinding against one another. Despite the hushed vibe in the room, they managed to remove each other's clothes with a measured rhythm, in a sultry, quiet, strip tease.

Julie's cream-colored, stretchy knit top was first to go. Now the girls were evenly matched as they touched and provoked one another in their close-fitting white bras and snug slacks. They had their hands on and around each other's breasts, playful fingers sliding beneath bra straps, tugging on them, pulling at them, flirting with them.

The bras were soon dispatched to the floor. Jack contemplated the modest mound of milk-hued lingerie as it lay by his feet. He wanted to look at the girl's exposed breasts for the first time; they were available, at eye level, just a foot or so away—but he couldn't—not yet. There was something so warm, so erotic, and so intoxicating about the small pile of delicate straps, cups, and clasps that rested close to his toes. It was only an overpriced stack of machine-sewn materials, but it represented much more to Jack. It marked the beginning of new relationships, new bonds—new levels of intimacy.

The girl's swaying feet and polished toes severed Jack from his trance, drawing his attention from their tossed-aside lingerie to the curves of their well-defined calves. He traced up the girl's tight pants, up past the smoldering creases between their thighs, up above the limits of the woven fabric—up where it was only skin.

Their bellies were flat, smooth, and inviting. Narrow lines of muscle angled down from above each of their hips, converging and spilling together in the small gap between their legs.

"Like what you see, Jack?" Cherry smiled, her grin wider, toothier, than Jack could recall it ever being.

Jack wanted to answer. He wanted to tell both of them that they were beautiful in every sense of the word. He wanted to beg them to remove their pants, so he could finally see, and taste, and fuck their precious little gashes. Instead, he sat in his chair glaring at their perfect tits, his mind and prick stunned, and frozen.

Four distinct exemplars of nature's finest pointed at Jack, stared at him, muted him. Cherry's breasts were as full and fleshy as Jack had imagined, although with Cherry there had never been much doubt about their dimension, shape, or ability to impress. Her nipples were small, tawny summits—focal points for otherwise unfathomable spheres.

Julie's nipples were quite a bit different from Cherry's. They seemed to soar from her firm, appropriately expansive tits, as if they were reaching for something, or someone. Where Cherry's breasts were satiny globes, Julie's were more sculpted, more defined. They didn't just rest on her chest—they seemed animated, buoyant.

"Can I have more...please?" Jack didn't want to beg—he had to. He wasn't sure how much more teasing his aching prick could bear.

"What do you think he wants more of?" Julie asked Cherry. "This?"

Julie's tongue stretched for one of Cherry's nipples. She sucked it into her mouth with a slurp, and let it roll across the surface of her glistening white teeth. Her palms cupped Cherry's heavy breasts, fondling them, molesting them. One of her hands drifted down Cherry's belly till it reached the split between her thighs. Her middle finger probed the gap, and, with intent, began to stroke her slit through the thin fabric. Cherry responded with an upturned head and muffled sighs.

Julie released Cherry from her mouth and turned toward her boss. "Is this what you wanted more of, Jack?"

"That's not what he wanted, Julie." Cherry seemed done with the games. Her skin was flushed, and the pitch of her voice was higher, almost squeaky. "He wanted this."

Cherry reached for the stamped-metal button at the top of her pants. Her thumbs slid inside the waistband, and she began to wriggle. Julie licked her lips then followed Cherry's lead.

Jack's patience had worn past thin. He slid off his chair and fell to his knees in front of Julie. He wasn't going to wait any longer. "Let me do it, girls—please let me."

With both hands, Jack yanked Julie's pants to the floor. Where he had expected to find a pair of delicate panties—another layer, another foiling irritation—there was just Julie. Julie, his little buttoned-down goody two shoes, fully waxed, ready to go. Jack's eyes, his nose, his mouth, were all inches from her, close enough to spy the dew on her folds and breathe from her simmering fire. He was also close enough to... taste her.

Jack wrapped his hands behind her silky, taut ass and pulled her to his mouth. His tongue probed her slit and hunted down her clit. He licked and he nibbled, and he sucked in her juices, savoring every drop of her bittersweet honey. Julie's whimpers became groans, and

Jack knew she was close. But he wasn't going to let her off that easy; not after the way he'd been tortured. It was someone else's turn.

Cherry had already worked her pants down her legs and off her feet. She had been watching, waiting, purring. Jack crawled like an anxious puppy to the familiar crease between her thighs. He'd seen it before, a thousand times, but not like this—not unsheathed, not this understandable.

"I want the same," Cherry murmured. "I want the same."

Jack considered her request, or demand, for about a second. He wanted to pleasure her as she had pleasured him. He wanted to dive into her pussy and stay there until they were both breathless. But his throbbing prick was screaming to him, and he couldn't ignore it.

Jack's eyes shot to an opened box of assorted sweaters that sat in the corner of his office. They were samples sent from his buyer buddy, Riley Duberman, who was seeking an honest opinion from a trusted manager. It was time to evaluate the contents.

With a quick shake of the box, Jack had the sweaters dumped into a pile on the floor. He spread them out in front of his desk, creating a thick, beastly looking blanket.

"Come here, girls." Jack commanded them; his erection pleaded with them.

"Hey, Julie—he's telling us where to come. We have to do what he says, right?"

"I'm ready. Let's do it…or him."

Jack was in charge, and he let the girls know. "Both of you—on your hands and knees, facing the same direction, next to each other."

The girls scrambled into position—giggling—ready.

Jack was ready, too. He kneeled behind them so he could see everything at once. It was the perfect rear view mirror—without the mirror.

The two bobbing butts yawned at him, affording a sneak preview of what he'd gotten himself into, or, more accurately, what he'd be getting himself into. Floating, silky knobs of blossoming sexuality nestled majestically between the rifts of their behinds. A pouting furrow coursed up and down the imploring ripe bulges, opening views to crooked inner folds. Atop the crowded furrow, thin pucker lines gathered around more confined, more restricted openings.

Both bottoms were soft, yet firm—small, yet feminine. He

M.L. Joslyn

wanted them both, and he would have them both. But, for now, he would take the one that he'd been fantasizing about the longest, the one he was sure he would never have.

Jack wormed his way behind Julie and wedged his knees between hers, nudging her legs apart—just enough. His hand dropped to her slit, and he followed her contours with one finger. As he grazed her lips, they opened full for him. He traced her inner creases, up and down, brushing her clit with each pass. She was so wet, and he was so ready.

With one hand Jack guided his stiff, throbbing cock into Julie's welcoming lair. He clutched her narrow, soft hips and pulled her back to him. The rhythm began as his length snuck deeper with each stroke. He glided and coasted inside her slippery, snug path until they had found their balance, their oneness. Jack wanted to give her more. He wanted to reach under her and fondle her swaying breasts. He wanted to stroke her clit, her thighs, her ass. But there was something else he wanted, and someone else that wanted him.

Cherry was still on her hands and knees, but she'd inched even closer to Julie. She had been rocking and swaying alongside her, keeping the tempo, feeling the heat. Their hips, their thighs, and their angled arms rubbed against each other, teased each other.

Cherry had made it easy for Jack to play with her too. Her ass was at his side, and he pressed his hand against it and then squeezed it, kneaded it. Soon his fingers had found their way inside her slick pussy—one at first—then a couple more. The rhythm of his fingers quickly matched the rhythm of his cock. The threesome had caught the same wave, but the beach was closing in fast. Jack had another thought.

As if they were inside each other's minds, they separated from one another at once. Jack clutched a handful of sweaters, fashioned a small pillow, and then laid on his back, head elevated, his erection scanning the room for attention. Cherry found his beating pole, polished it once to feel its slickness, and then climbed aboard. She squeezed the head of his dick with her tight snatch and then let her slight frame ease slowly onto him. Her weighty breasts were close enough for him to handle, close enough for him to molest. He lifted them in his palms to feel their heft. He ran his thumbs over the swollen nipples as Cherry found her tempo.

Jack glanced at Julie, and she knew what he wanted—what they

68

both wanted. Quickly, her strong thighs straddled Jack's mouth, her back grazing Cherry's bouncing breasts, her hands dancing through Jack's thick brown hair.

Cherry braced herself with her hands on Julie's waist, and she leaned in further, her nipples buffing, seemingly fucking, Julie's narrow back. They found their beat again, their well-oiled rhythm. Cherry's strong thighs levered her body from Jack, her pussy sucking his cock as she rose and assaulting it as she plunged. She rode every inch of his length, savoring every ridge, and every swell. Julie pitched forward and back just faintly, governing and controlling her ride, guiding her most sensitive parts over Jack's warm lips and exploring tongue.

Jack's arms were filled with Julie's firm ass, one hand working each cheek, separating the round bubbles, squeezing them together, probing the space between. His mouth was filled with Julie's sweet snatch, catching the parts he could as she rocked over him, thrusting his tongue anywhere there was a space. His dick was filled with Cherry, who was working his shaft so well, so skillfully, so…effectively.

A groundswell of warm, sticky cream gathered low in Jack's gut, in the crawlspace behind his prick. It waited for a signal. It waited for all sense and reason and judgment to come to a halt so it could storm from his quivering body. It waited for a nod.

When Cherry's clenching pussy tumbled to his lap and hesitated—when Julie's engorged clit paused over his flicking tongue—when the girl's cries of ecstasy sailed in harmony to the ceiling—the switch tripped.

Jack, Julie, and Cherry all came hard, and they all came at once. Jack's prick thickened past full, and then erupted with rolling swells of milky nectar that charged deep inside Cherry's shuddering tunnel. Julie's snatch spilled a flood of sweet juices into Jack's persistent mouth, and over his innocent chin. The peaks, the waves, and the rushes of their orgasms built fast, and then fell slow.

Shallow-breathed, intertwined bodies smothered the makeshift blanket of spoiled sweaters below them. They were spent—and content.

"Are we still open?" Jack asked, not wanting to hear the answer.

"We're open anytime you want, Jack," Julie whispered, arms

M.L. Joslyn

stretched above her head, legs loosely braided with Cherry's.

"Jack, I'll lock up tonight," Cherry said. "Why don't you go home."

"No way, Cherry. You girls leave. I can handle this. Besides, Carrie can take care of the sales floor. I'll just get some work done in here—maybe tidy up a bit."

"Um…I think I might have told Carrie she can leave a little early tonight," Cherry said. "She has a, uh, date."

"You're letting Carrie go home early because she has a date?" Julie asked. "That's probably not a…"

"She's going out with Joel, Julie. Don't ask."

"Are you fucking kidding me?" Jack asked, chuckling to himself. "That's great. Let her go. And you girls go, too. It's probably better if we didn't all leave at the same time, anyway. Seriously—I can handle this myself."

"You can handle lots of things, Jack," Cherry said. "Alright, if you insist."

***

Jack leaned back in his desk chair, scanning his office for remnants, or evidence, of the most awesome—the most startling—sexual experience of his life. The room was clean, but his mind was filled with dirty, indecent thoughts. He wanted to keep them there for a while, relish them, and bask in them.

Thirty more minutes and he could lock the doors and head for the relative sanity and comfortable mattress awaiting him at home. He looked at his watch again, riveted by the second hand as it pulsed around the dial. The hypnotic spell was broken when he was paged to pick up line two.

"Jack Timmons—may I help you?"

"Hi Jack—Mike Allen, your favorite DM. How's business?"

"Hey, Mike. Business is great. You do read the sales reports I send you every day, right? What are you doing working so late, anyway? I thought you had like a nine to two job."

"I love your sense of humor, Jack. Just one of the things I love about you. Listen, I had a call earlier from corporate."

"I swear, it wasn't me, whatever happened."

70

"Ha-ha. Look, I had to think about this for a while before I called you. I wasn't sure I wanted to, um, talk to you about it. Then, I decided that just because you're my best store manager I couldn't be selfish about this thing."

"Mike—what the hell are you talking about?"

"Corporate, or, I guess, we, would like to promote you, Jack. How do you feel about living in New York?"

"What?"

"You'd be an Associate Buyer—for now. Once you learn the ropes, it's a pretty fast track to buyer. It's a great opportunity for you Jack—lots more money—a few more perks. Don't give me an answer now. I want you to think about it. Okay?"

"Okay, Mike."

"You'll have lots of questions. Call me tomorrow and we'll talk."

"Thanks, Mike. Your best store manager, huh?"

"Don't tell anyone I said that. Oh, and remember, you'll get to live in New York—the most exciting city in the world, Jack. Bye."

Jack exhaled with a sigh. He looked around his office with a different eye than he'd used a few moments earlier. What a day, he thought.

It was too difficult for him to sit at his desk. It was time for a pre-closing walk-through of the store, anyway. He gathered himself together and headed across the sales floor.

There were just a couple shoppers sifting through the sales fixtures. The only other people in the store were a few employees straightening things, getting the place ready for the next morning. Jack nodded at them and pointed toward the fitting rooms. Yes, they were empty, and yes they were clean, the two part-timers implied with their thumbs in the air.

Jack strolled through the racks, making sure everything was neat and presentable. He glanced over at the fitting rooms, checking to see if the curtains were pulled back and secured, a sure sign they were unoccupied.

When the last of the browsing stragglers had left, it was time to shut the place down. Jack instructed his one remaining cashier to close out her drawer, and asked the rest of the staff to scout around once more, just to make sure everything was orderly.

Mike's offer kept circling through Jack's head. He didn't know what to do. If he were to grow with the company, New York was the place to be. *You'll get to live in New York—the most exciting city in the world, Jack.* He wasn't expecting to have to make a decision like this—at least not for a long time.

With the flip of a finger, Jack dimmed the store lighting by half. The sales floor was still bright enough for his employees to finish with their work, yet shadowy enough to keep latecomers from rattling the locked doors. He took one more pass around the perimeter, assuring the store was secure and tidy.

As he was passing fitting room one he thought he heard something fall to the floor, like maybe a precariously balanced hanger had lost its grip. The curtain had been pulled away from the entrance and fastened back with a corded rope. Jack poked his head in and scanned for the culprit.

Just inside the entry, a very attractive, very well dressed middle-aged woman, stood with her eyes on Jack, a cheerful smile across her face. She had her left hand on the shoulder of a much younger version of herself. Jack guessed the girl to be about twenty.

The girl was nude, save for a pair of thong-style white panties. Her long blonde hair fell evenly to both sides of her head, courtesy of a crisp, unswerving part. Her flickering blue eyes, pouty red lips, and perfect set of full, firm breasts qualified her as a possible runway model. The girl's smile couldn't have been brighter, or wider.

"I'm so sorry. I had no idea we still had customers."

"Oh, I blame myself for taking so long," the middle-aged woman said. "Carrie told us it wouldn't be a problem if we stayed a little after hours. I really appreciate it. I'm helping my daughter pick out an interview outfit. We have to get this right; it's her dream job. Isn't that exciting?"

"That is very exciting," Jack answered, wondering why she didn't seem the least unnerved by a strange man leering at her naked daughter. "Good luck with your interview. It's hard to find a good job doing something you love."

Before Jack left the room, he glanced once more at the girl's bold nipples. They pointed at him, like they were trying to tell him something.

Jack closed the fitting room curtain behind him and walked with purpose across the sales floor. He had to ask a couple of his employees to stick around a little. There was more work to be done, more customer service to provide. He'd take care of what he was supposed to. And then he'd get to come back tomorrow.

The End

www.ingramcontent.com/pod-product-compliance
Lightning Source LLC
Chambersburg PA
CBHW070351130626
46556CB00007B/3132

9781630662912